The Cats That Stalked a Ghost

Karen Anne Golden

D1377856

Copyright

Dedication

To

Max and Dee Dee

Pooky

Pee Wee and Iris

Table of Contents

Prologue

"No-o-o," Katherine screamed, waking up. She sat up on the cot, sweat pouring off her brow. *I was having the worst nightmare.* But then she thought she heard a cat wail. It sounded like her Siamese cat, Scout. *That's impossible. I'm hallucinating.* But something was outside the door, jiggling the exterior latch to the abandoned storm cellar.

"Help me," she called in a weak voice. "I can't get out."

"Waugh," Scout cried.

Katherine got up and slowly climbed the steps until her head nearly touched the cellar doors. She swallowed hard and bit back tears. "This isn't happening. I'm dreaming again."

Scout muttered something in Siamese, and went back to jiggling the latch.

1

Katherine heard the sound of metal scraping, and then a thump on the ground. She took her cue, pushed the left-hand door, and opened it. She picked up Scout and hugged her. "I love you, sweet girl."

Katherine squinted and adjusted her eyes to the daylight. Glancing at the burned-out shell of a two-story building, she wondered where she was. Behind her was an overgrown yard, with a rusted barbed wire fence in front. She could make out weathered tombstones; some of them had toppled to the ground. When she looked back at the building, an apparition appeared behind a glassless window. First, the figure pointed to the cemetery, then gestured toward a dirt lane that went around the building.

Scout chattered, "At-at-at-at!" Her long, pencil-thin tail quivered against Katherine's side.

"You see her, too," Katherine whispered, relieved that she wasn't seeing things. "It's going to be okay, Scout." She was too frightened to speak any louder. Then the spirit disappeared.

2

Chapter One

Katherine "Katz" Kendall, heiress to a fortune, wasn't your stereotypical "high-maintenance" millionaire. You could count on one hand the number of reasons why she didn't fit into the new-to-wealth model.

First, Katherine didn't need the money to live comfortably. She had a computer sciences degree, and a stellar work history in Manhattan. Second, she didn't seek fame, nor did she want to be a celebrity. She was a private person, happy to live a modest life with a few, select friends. Third, she wasn't a material girl. She didn't own an expensive car, dress in designer clothes, or drip in diamond jewelry.

What set Katherine apart from the norm, and moved her to the head of her class, was her attitude: she genuinely cared about other people. She'd give the shirt off her back to help the disadvantaged. She secretly sought out the needy — those who were too proud to ask for help — and she'd anonymously get them back on their feet financially.

When Katherine's great-aunt, Orvenia Colfax, passed away, she willed most of her estate to a relative she'd never met. Katherine was the daughter of Orvenia's niece and lived in New York City. Orvenia lived in the small town of Erie, Indiana, northwest of Indianapolis. She went through several wills, but ultimately left millions to her twenty-six-year-old great-niece.

Katherine also inherited a seventeen-room, pink Victorian mansion, and a golden-eyed Abyssinian cat named Abigail. She already had three cats of her own, two seal points, and a lilac-point Siamese. Because she loved cats, the inheritance made it easier for her to give up living in the big city and move to the Midwest. Since then, she'd met the love of her life, Jake Cokenberger, a history professor at the City University. The couple had recently adopted two male Siamese kittens.

Today was Friday, and Katherine's last computer training class. She sat behind a desk, watching her last student collect his belongings.

"Thanks for everything," he said, as he stopped and came over to her desk. "Hey, Ms. Kendall, I'd like to take the advanced class."

"You're quite welcome, Anthony. You scored very well on the tests," Katherine said. "I'll put your name in for next session's lottery." She offered training at a minimum price, so townspeople could find better jobs. So many sent in applications, Katherine had to devise a lottery to select four names for each class. She didn't mention that two of her cats did the final drawing. She'd write the candidates' names on an index card, fold it, and throw each card into a large glass bowl. Then her two Siamese, Scout and Abra, would pull out several cards, play with them, and bless the winning candidates with a fang-marked edge.

"Great," Anthony smiled. "Oh, I guess I should ask, when is the next session?"

5

"The advanced class starts in November. I'm taking a few months off —"

"To get married to Jake Cokenberger," he finished boldly. "Congratulations! That's way too cool, taking a long honeymoon."

Katherine laughed. "Actually, we're not. Jake doesn't get a break from the university until December." She thought the student was too nosy, but all the townspeople were just like him. They never felt too timid to ask a personal question.

She kept it to herself that Jake and she would initially take a short, romantic holiday to coincide with Jake's fall break, with plans for a longer vacation later, to include the cats. But the student didn't need to know this.

"I'll be off then. Thanks again." The young man walked out the door, and closed it behind him. Katherine got up, walked over, and locked it. She began tidying the workstations, stashing training manuals underneath the top of the desks, in their special cubbyholes.

Scout and Abra — seal-point Siamese sisters — trotted in and began their daily inspection. Judging from the cobwebs on their noses, it was apparent they'd already checked out other rooms in the basement. Now with the students gone, they did a quick once-over around the classroom.

Abra was interested in the smell wafting from under the exterior door. She stretched up and stood very tall on hind legs. She held her jaw slightly open and flared her nostrils. Scout joined her and did the same thing. They looked like they just stepped off the set of *Meerkat Manor*. They both sniffed disapprovingly.

"It's smoke, my treasures. I hope there isn't another house fire." She peered out the window and scanned the back yard, making sure the carriage house wasn't ablaze, or one of her neighbors' houses. She startled as the town-wide fire siren began wailing its warning for volunteers to rush to the station.

Scout growled at the loud sound.

Someone pounded loudly on the door, and Katherine moved from the window. She wondered who it might be, thinking a student had left something behind. She looked out the door's security viewer, recognized who it was, and opened the door.

"Hi, Cokey," she said to her handyman.

Cokey stood outside, clutching two buckets. Scout made a mad dash for the door, but Katherine caught her. "Hey, you, you're not going out," she said adamantly. Then to Cokey, "I'm sorry. Come in. I've got to take these two rascals upstairs before another one tries to escape," she said, seizing Abra as well.

"No problem," Cokey said. "I'll make my way to the back."

"Give me a sec," Katherine said, taking the Siamese upstairs to her back office. The cats squirmed to be free. "Quit it," she scolded. "Scout, I don't want you to go outside. There are all sorts of dangers lurking out there." She carried the cats into the office, past her computer desk, and into an all-season sun porch. She set the cats down.

"Waugh," the Siamese sassed, then jumped on Abra, biting her sister on the ear.

"Brat! Stop that!"

Abra squealed and turned, punching Scout with the equivalent of her left hook. The two wrestled for a split-second, stopped, and began grooming each other.

"Cats! To think I have seven of them," Katherine muttered, returning to the basement.

Cokey stood by the water heater, dumping the contents of a small waste basket into a two-wheeled garbage cart. "Hey Katz, what's with Scout tryin' to run out? Usually when I come over, she's too interested in what I'm doin' to even think about runnin' outside."

"Last July, when I was at the cabin and totally out of it, Scout got a taste of being outside. Both Scout and Abra explored the area, and even went catfishing in the pond."

Cokey grinned. "Scout got her adventure fix, and it sounds like she wants more. Maybe you should buy a leash and take her on walks."

"You read my mind. I just ordered seven harnesses and leashes online."

Cokey continued grinning. "You're taking seven cats for a walk at the same time?"

"No, I think I'll start with Scout." Katherine giggled.

"Margie and I tried the leash thing with our cat, Spitfire, but the orange lug collapsed on the carpet, and acted like we were trying to kill him or somethin'. He wouldn't budge until we took the dang thing off."

"Too funny," Katherine said, then changed the subject. "I wonder where the fire is?"

"Considering the smoke in the air, I'd say pretty close. I wouldn't worry about it. Probably someone burned lunch," Cokey said, trying to make light of the situation. Recently the small town of Erie had its share of mysterious fires, probably intentionally started. Because the town had been besieged by an arsonist in the past, everyone, including the fire chief, prayed another firebug hadn't been born.

"I hope not, either. I read in the paper that the serial arsonist's trial is coming up."

"It's a shame. Max Taylor is only eighteen-years-old. I know his parents. They hired the best attorney — they've got money, they can do that," Cokey digressed.

"Max got his kicks setting fire to abandoned farm buildings. I think he burned twenty to the ground."

"What do you mean by burn to the ground? Didn't the fire department put them out?"

"You gotta remember. Out in the country, the building could be beyond saving before anyone knew it was on fire, especially at night when people were asleep, and didn't see the smoke, or smell it."

"I take it he set all the fires at night?"

"Yep. Right now Max's parents' greatest concern is the judge."

"Why?" Katherine asked inquisitively.

"Everyone in these parts calls Judge Hartman the hanging judge. She'll show no mercy."

Katherine wondered if Cokey had been in front of this judge before, but didn't comment. Cokey had his own troubles with the law, but that was in his past. Instead, she asked, "Did you know Judge Hartman is going to preside over our wedding?"

Cokey's face dropped in shock, then he quickly recovered. "I had no idea."

Katherine noticed the change in expression and tried to steer the conversation somewhere else. "So how are the bookcases coming along?" Cokey was building bookcases for Jake's large book collection.

"Here, I'll show you," Cokey said, motioning her back to his work area. Katherine followed him.

"I'm using premium, quarter-sawn oak," he said, picking up one of the boards. I have one more bookcase to build, and then Margie and I are going to stain them."

"That will be perfect. Jake's using this part of the basement as his office."

"Oh, I should let ya know, we'll be using an oil-based stain, so you might smell it upstairs for a few days."

Katherine eyes widened. "Seriously, Cokey? I don't want the house to smell to beat the band during my wedding."

"I'll have the windows open down here. Plus I'll run a fan. Shouldn't be a problem."

"Okay, thanks," Katherine said, turning to leave. "I'll be upstairs if you need me."

Chapter Two

Katherine breathed a sigh of relief that her busy weekend was over. Last-minute wedding plans were getting on her nerves.

She walked out the basement exterior door and marveled how blue the sky was, with not a cloud in sight. The trees hadn't turned yet, but the air was getting colder. *Perfect weather for a short bike ride around Erie*, she thought. Heading to the carriage house, she unlocked the padlock and slid the door open. Inside, she lifted her Huffy cruiser bike off the wall-rack and wheeled it to the driveway.

Stevie Sanders, son of Erie's crime boss, drove up in a shiny black Dodge Ram and parked. The logo "Stevie's Electrical" was painted on his driver-side door. He'd put the same logo on a front vanity plate. He got out and walked over. With a seductive glint in his eyes and a handsome smile, he said, "Long time, no see, good lookin'.

I've been meanin' to stop by and say howdy, but most of my work has been out in the boonies."

"Hi, Stevie," Katherine said, surprised to see him. "I seem to remember the last time I saw you, you helped me plant daylilies."

"Did they make it?" he snickered.

"Yes, but they didn't flower."

"They will next year. Hey, I've got a job next door at Mrs. Harper's. Is it okay if I park here? I'm rewiring her basement for a new furnace."

"Yes, of course. Nice seeing you," she said, getting on her bike.

"Wait, can I have a word," Stevie said, striking a match and lighting a cigarette. He threw the match on the drive, then picked it up. "Sorry, didn't mean to be a litterbug."

"Okay," Katherine said, getting off her bike. "What is it you want to talk to me about?"

"I'm truly sorry about the events last July at Leonard's place. I've been meanin' to tell ya, and you probably heard this from my sister, Barbie, but we *were* tryin' to help you, but we didn't know you were stayin' at the cabin. Cousin Jimmy was armed, and because of the storm and stuff, it was too dangerous."

"I know. I understand," Katherine smiled.

Stevie said with a flirty tone, "I can't think of anyone else I'd like savin' — "

Katherine cut him off. "It's been nice to see you, Stevie, but I've got a meeting to go to, and I need to drop off some letters at the post office."

"Ma'am, you take care now." He tipped his ball cap and walked back to his truck.

***

Several hours later, Katherine returned and walked her bike into the carriage house. She was happy Stevie's truck wasn't in the parking area. His flirtatious manner made her uncomfortable.

She extracted her cellphone from her jeans back pocket and sent Jake a text. "Where are you?" Jake was a half hour late. He was teaching at the university and his last class was at one p.m. Her cell rang and she hurried to accept it. "Hi, Jake," she said.

"Hey, Sweet Pea. I'm about a mile from Erie. Have you had lunch?"

"No, not yet. I just got back from my meeting with Dr. Goodwin."

"Who?"

"The new director of the Erie Animal Rescue Center — "

How'd it go?" Jake interrupted.

"Great. Dr. Goodwin has excellent credentials and is very personable."

"How personable? She or he?"

"He," Katherine giggled. "No worries, my love. He wasn't blessed in the looks department, but he's an excellent veterinarian."

"You mean he can eat apples through a picket fence?"

She laughed. "Where do you come up with these things?"

"I'm a natural-born Hoosier."

"Speaking of apples — food — the meeting ran a bit late and I had to bicycle back, so to make a long story short, I'm starving."

"I'll pick up some fried chicken at the deli. Mashed potatoes and coleslaw sound okay?"

"Yes, my mouth is watering. Could you do me a favor?"

"I'm always at your beck and call," he said playfully.

"I like that," she answered affectionately. "When you get here, can you park behind the mansion? I thought it would be fun to eat at the picnic table. I know it's a bit nippy today, but soon it will be too cold to be outside at all."

"Sounds good to me. I've been cooped up in a classroom all morning, and I'm a little stir crazy. Being outside sounds like a mighty fine idea."

"Great! See you in a minute."

"Sure thing," he said, disconnecting the call.

Katherine walked to a bank of storage cabinets that lined the south interior wall of the carriage house, and pulled out place mats. She headed to the picnic table and set them down. The wind picked up one and blew it across the yard. "Dang it," she said, chasing after it. It landed on the ground outside the classroom. Overhead, on the all-season sun porch, she felt eyes staring at her. She looked up to see seven curious cats looking down. Dewey, a seal-point kitten, began climbing the screen.

"Stop that!" Katherine scolded.

Crowie, the other seal-point kitten, did the same.

"Get down," Katherine said in her I-mean-business voice.

"Mao," Dewey cried with surprising volume. The kitten had the voice of a baritone. He unhooked his claws and fell to the windowsill. Crowie did the same. Iris jumped up between the two and began washing Dewey's ears. Miss Siam had finally found a buddy.

Katherine returned to the picnic table and set the place mat down. She grabbed the second one and held both of them down with her elbow while she waited for Jake.

After fifteen minutes, Jake drove up in the Jeep. He parked and climbed out. Walking over to the passenger side, he took out a large bag.

Katherine put her hand over her mouth to cover a laugh. Jake was wearing his John Dillinger's outfit. He taught a history course on Prohibition, and whenever he got to the part about organized crime, he dressed up like the famous 1930s Indiana gangster. "Teaching about the bad boys today?"

Jake winked.

"Did anyone at the deli notice your attire?"

"If they did, they didn't say anything." He leaned down and kissed Katherine on the top of her head.

"Actually, I never told you this before," she began, "but I think you look more like Johnny Depp in the movie than Dillinger."

"Yep, I've been told that. But I think you got it backwards. Johnny Depp looks like me," he said with a mischievous look in his eyes.

He tried to set the carry-out bag on the table, but a gust of wind prevented him from letting go of the handle.

"Wow," he said, clutching it. "It's gotten really breezy out. Want to go inside?"

"I have a cool idea. Let's eat in the carriage house. We've never done that before, and I wanted to talk to you about something without the cats overhearing."

"What?" he asked curiously. "You think your cats understand us when we talk?"

"Um, yes, my cats do. See them," she said, pointing up at the sun porch. "They're listening right now."

"Ma-waugh," Scout agreed.

"Hi, kids," Jake called up to them.

Katherine got up and grabbed two nearby plastic lawn chairs. Jake moved over, "Here, you take the sack and I'll carry the chairs."

"Okay, but it's a bag, not a sack."

"Maybe in New York, but not here." He took the chairs inside the carriage house and positioned them near an overturned empty crate. "We can use this as a table. What about forks and knives?"

"Got that covered, too," she said, returning to the storage cabinet and removing a picnic basket. "Within this basket is everything you'd ever need in a picnic emergency." She pulled out plastic forks and knives, and set them on the crate.

"Emergency picnic basket," he chuckled. "That works." From the carry-out bag, he lifted two Styrofoam food containers. He handed one to Katherine, as well as a stack of napkins.

Katherine immediately got the joke. She was notorious for spilling things on her clothes. "Very funny," she commented.

Jake opened his container and dove in.

Biting into the chicken, Katherine said, with her mouth full, "The cats have been busy surfing up scary things on the computer."

Jake laughed. "This ought to be interesting. Like what?"

"The hotel I booked in Chicago is on multiple floors, starting on the seventh. Their website was down, so the cats heard me making the reservation on the phone. Less than a half hour later, guess what was up on my computer screen?"

"Let me guess. Knowing your cats, something about hotel fires."

"Sort of. How about the old movie trailer for *The Towering Inferno*?"

"I take it you cancelled the reservation," Jake said, amused, but in awe of the extraordinariness of Katherine's cats.

"So, I searched on the Internet for a place we could stay, which wouldn't involve a super-long drive," she said in-between bites of coleslaw. "Pigeon Forge, Tennessee, is about eight hours from Erie. I was just about to book a mountain-view cabin that is so awesome, it even has a Jacuzzi."

"I've been to Pigeon Forge when I was a teenager. There's an amusement park nearby that's really fun. Lots of down home cookin' and music. We'll have to check that out."

Katherine shook her head. "Ah, not thinkin' so. The cats heard me talking about it to Margie, and guess what? A few hours later, I walk into my office and there on the screen was a gruesome photo of a mother bear protecting her cubs."

"Gruesome meaning a human was getting mauled?"

"Yes, afraid so."

"They're definitely bears in that neck of the woods, so let's nix that one, too. Besides, I don't relish driving eight hours there and back. That would really cut into our together time. Any other suggestions, or do we spend our honeymoon at the mansion with the cats, because I think that's what they want us to do."

"I'll try and locate a hotel near Chicago that's only a few stories high. Or should we stick with our original plan and stay near the Navy Pier?"

Jake shook his head. "No, if the cats surfed up those pages, we ought to heed their warning."

"Agreed."

"Listen, let me call a colleague of mine who teaches at the University of Chicago. Maybe he can suggest a hotel with lower floors?"

"And fire escapes," Katherine added, tearing off another piece of chicken.

Changing the subject, Jake asked, "Did you make the appointment with Dr. Sonny to neuter the kittens?"

"I didn't call from inside the mansion. I came out here and called him. Lord knows what would happen if the cats overheard *that* conversation, especially Iris. She's bonded so much to Dewey, I can imagine there will be a bit of separation anxiety."

"I'm so glad they hit it off. It's funny that Scout and Abra are littermates and best friends, but Dewey and Crowie aren't."

"That's okay, because Lilac and Abby have adopted Crowie. The climbing cat club has to stick together," Katherine laughed, remembering how at first the kittens thought Jake was a tree. Then she added, "Dr. Sonny is keeping Dewey and Crowie for several days, so we don't have to worry about them while we're gone. Plus, it will be two fewer cats for our pet sitter to take care of."

"I just saw Elsa at the deli. She was chatting up the Erie reporter guy, what's his name?"

"Russell Krow. He's our wedding photographer, silly goose, and you can't remember his name?"

"I do now, 'silly goose' right back at ya. Elsa is good at cat wrangling, but she's barkin' up the wrong tree with Russell. Folks at the diner said he's Erie's new Casanova."

Katherine made a face. "Yes, and everything the diner folks say is true."

Jake teased, "Just like the Internet."

Chapter Three

Sitting on an Eastlake side chair, Katherine sat in the atrium, studying the guest list for the wedding reception. A few minutes earlier, Jake's mom, Cora Cokenberger, had hand-delivered the list. She didn't stay long because she was allergic to cats. The kittens — Dewie and Crowie — didn't get that memo, and kept jumping on her lap, while Iris tried to steal things from her Vera Bradley bag. Between sneezes, Cora raved that most of the invitees had RSVP'd, and were delighted to attend.

The previous month, Katherine had given her future mother-in-law free rein to host the reception, as long as she had nothing to do with planning the wedding itself. However, she did convince Cora to invite guests the couple knew, and not everyone in the State of Indiana. Katherine could count on two hands the number of people she was acquainted with in town, but Cora seemed to know every single man, woman, and child in Erie and the surrounding counties.

The reception was being held in the armory that had been built in 1931 with WPA funds. It was the site of the famous cake auction where Lilac — flying Siamese — leveled the cake table, including Cora's famous volcano cake. Back in December, the committee for the annual charity event had sent Katherine a snippy letter stating both Lilac and she were banned from attending another function. Katherine wondered how much Cora paid the committee under the table to allow Jake and her to have their reception there. *Probably plenty*, she surmised, e*ither in money or cakes*. If it were left to the happy couple, they'd prefer a less-conspicuous setting with fewer people, but Katherine wanted to please her future mother-in-law, so she acquiesced.

Studying the list, she noticed that most of the attendees were Cokenbergers. Jake had a huge extended family, led by Grandpa Cokenberger, who was so entertaining, he could be a stand-up comedian. Scanning through the names, she finally came to people she knew.

Mark Dunn, the former estate attorney for her late great-aunt, was coming with Detective Linda Martin. They'd become quite an item. Katherine was happy about that.

When she read "Mrs. Murphy and Guest," she said out loud, "What? Mum is bringing a guest. I wonder who it is?" Mum's son, Jacky — Colleen's youngest brother — was attending, but his name was already on the list. Jacky was flying out of LaGuardia Airport in a few days, but brothers Jimmy and Joey sent their regrets. Katherine thought that was okay, because she really didn't know Jimmy and Joey very well. They were ten years older and hung around with their own crowd.

She continued reading. "Marcia Harper Smith and Guest send their regrets." Cora didn't know the story about Evan Hamilton — the Vietnam veteran who had saved her life two months earlier. Katherine knew that Marcia and Evan were going to be in Indy that weekend. Evan had an appointment with a prosthetic eye surgeon.

Mid-way through the list, she spotted a name she wasn't familiar with — Veronica Lake. *The 1940s movie star*, Katherine thought, then read the penciled-in comment next to Veronica's name, written by Cora herself: "Victoria's mom is not able to attend."

"Oh no, she didn't," Katherine said, shocked. "She invited Jake's deceased wife's mother? Why would she do that?" Katherine had never met Victoria's mom. Jake said she kept to herself and didn't attend many social events. Katherine thought, *If she would have come, that would have been so awkward.*

Katherine's cell rang and she slid the bar to answer. "Yes," she said, sounding annoyed.

"Chief London here. Katz, you got a minute?"

Katherine calmed down. "Yes, of course. What can I help you with?"

"Are you home?"

"Yes."

33

"Can you meet me out front? I'm pulling up right now."

"Sure," Katherine answered. She wondered what on earth the chief had to tell her in person that couldn't be said on the phone. Then the hair stood up on the back of her neck. She started to panic. *Did something bad happen to Jake? Was he in a car accident?* She flew to the front door, opened it, and hurried out.

The chief met her on the sidewalk. "I'll cut right to the chase. We've had a number of suspicious fires this month. The fire inspector suspects foul play."

"Why would anyone do such a thing?" she asked, shuddering at the thought.

"This town has always been full of fire bugs. Last year we caught the arsonist who was torching barns out in the country. He's up for trial next week."

"I heard about that, but he's in jail, so it couldn't be him."

"Last night, Becky's Antique Store burned. Firefighters were able to put it out before any of the neighboring buildings' caught on fire. It's a mess. Our volunteer fire department has really been taxed. We just don't have the manpower to keep up with this."

"I'm sorry to hear that," Katherine said, then made a mental note to do something about that situation.

"I'll get to the point. The buildings downtown are on the national register of historic places."

"I hope Becky's Antique Store can be rebuilt, but the antiques are gone forever."

"Katz, be on the lookout, and report anything suspicious around your house. Your Queen Anne Victorian would be an ideal target for an arsonist."

"I will, Chief. Thanks for stopping by and telling me in person." She respected the fact that the chief was a bona fide worrywart, and always one step ahead of the game.

"Katz," he said, tipping his police chief hat. "Watch your back."

She nodded.

The chief got into his cruiser, and drove east on Lincoln Street.

Katherine turned to go back inside the house, but two Siamese looking out the parlor picture window caught her attention. Inside on the windowsill, Abra stretched tall on her rear haunches, and with her front paws dangling, assumed her new Meerkat pose; Scout was sitting next to her, clearly agitated. Both wore troubled expressions on their brown masks.

Katherine went inside to comfort them, and was amazed at how quickly the Siamese made it to the door. "Back, back," she said, putting her foot up in case Scout flung out. She hurried in and shut the heavy oak door. "You two are fast."

"Waugh," Scout cried, rubbing against her leg. Katherine picked her up and kissed her on the head. Abra reached up to be held. "Okay, how about I sit on the floor for a group hug." She set Scout down, and hugged the two cats. "It's okay," she comforted. "We're safe here. No one is going to try and hurt us." She mouthed the words, but was worried. A distant memory ran through her head.

When she was younger, and lived with her parents in Brooklyn, the attic floor of their townhouse caught on fire. She'd remembered waking up to the blaring alarm, the smell of smoke, and her parents rousing her from her bed. Her father carried Katherine downstairs, while her mom opened the front door to safety. Even though the firefighters had quickly put out the flames, Katherine couldn't extinguish the memory.

Chapter Four

Katherine walked into the cat's playroom and gazed happily at the cats. Scout and Abra were sharing a cozy bed on the perch of a cat tree. Nearby, Lilac, Abby and Crowie were snuggled in another bed, while Iris and Dewey cuddled in the third.

"Ahhh," she cooed. "You kids are way too cute." She reached in her back pocket and extracted her cell. She clicked several pictures of her cats, planning to use one for her monitor's desktop background.

Scout jumped off the cat tree, stretched, and sharpened her claws on the sisal-covered post. Abra did the same.

Katherine said to Abra, "I need to borrow your sister for a minute."

"Raw," Abra protested.

Katherine gathered Scout in her arms, walked downstairs, and carried her to the front door. Abra followed, voicing her displeasure in a loud, catly way.

"Next time, Abra, but Scout gets to go first." Earlier,

Katherine had placed the nylon harness on Scout, so she'd

get used to it before the walk. She was amazed that Scout

didn't mind wearing it. She attached the leash and walked

out the door. Abra ran out, too.

"No, you can't come." Holding Scout with one

hand, she caught Abra with the other, and set her inside the

house.

Walking down the porch steps, Katherine could

hear Abra having a complete, royal Siamese cat fit behind

the door.

Katherine leaned down and set Scout on the

sidewalk. The seal point trotted several feet, then collapsed

on her side. She began rolling back-and-forth.

"Scout, what are you doing? We're taking a walk."

She slightly nudged the Siamese with the toe of her

sneaker. Scout jumped up and walked several more feet. Then Scout spotted a grassy area, and she lunged for it.

"Enough," Katherine reprimanded. "I know this isn't your first rodeo, so get moving."

"Na-waugh," Scout cried, snatching a blade of grass and chewing on it.

Katherine admitted to herself that Scout's first walk on the leash was proving to be a challenge. Scout alternated between trotting a few feet, and collapsing on the grass with her blue eyes slightly crossed in pure feline ecstasy.

"Scout, this is killing my back having to reach down to pick you up," Katherine complained.

The Siamese totally ignored her and rolled on her back. Kicking her back legs, she cried a loud series of Siamese complaints.

"Okay, that's it. We're going back inside." When Katherine tried to pick up the sassy Siamese, Scout dug her front claws into the grass. "Let go," she said, grabbing a paw and trying to unhook five entangled claws.

Scout released her claws and charged toward the yellow brick American Foursquare next door to the mansion. During Prohibition, the house had a speakeasy in the basement, and a tunnel that connected it to the mansion. The previous year, Katherine's great-uncle's skeleton had been found in the tunnel.

"Scout, slow down."

A dark gray Ford Taurus pulled up and a silver-haired woman got out. "Are you Katherine?" the woman asked.

Katherine noted the logo on the passenger-side door — Erie Realty.

"Yes, and you are?" she asked, as she picked up Scout and held her in her arms.

"I'm Ava Franklin. I'm a Realtor with Erie Realty; been there over twenty years."

41

"How may I help you?" Katherine asked, suspecting Ava wanted more than to stop by and chat.

"I heard through the grapevine that you've let the listing on this house expire. I stopped by to let you know I'm available in case you want to relist it."

"Let's talk," Katherine said. "Would you like to go inside the house and take a look-see?"

"Sure, I'd love to."

Katherine directed the way with Scout struggling in her arms to be set free. "Quit it!" she said sternly.

Ava looked perplexed. "Quit what?"

"I'm sorry. I was talking to my cat. She's not being very cooperative today. This is our first time taking a walk on a leash. She'd much rather walk me."

The realtor laughed. "I've gotta admit, this is the first time I've ever seen anyone walk a cat."

Stepping up to the porch, Katherine rummaged for her key ring with one hand while holding Scout with the other. She opened the door. "Come in."

Ava stepped into the house and her jaw dropped. "This is fabulous!"

Katherine shut the door. "I'm going to let my cat roam the house," she said, removing the leash. Scout darted into the main living room, and began her reconnaissance mission to scan-and-sniff every nook and cranny.

Katherine explained, "The Foursquare was built in the early 1920s, and belonged to my great-aunt Orvenia Colfax. Last February, I inherited this house from her estate. Margie Cokenberger did the restoration, and did a super job."

Ava admired. "I like the way the modern meets the old. The walls are a nice neutral color, and the original, stained woodwork really complements them."

Katherine agreed. "Let's head back to the kitchen."

Ava stepped into the room. "Fantastic," she commented. "In my business, the kitchen is the number one room to improve."

"Stainless steel appliances, granite countertops, island, 42-inch cherry cabinets — "

Ava interrupted, "and the most gorgeous oak floors."

"They're original. Margie's team sanded and stained them."

Katherine showed Ava the rest of the house. Midway through the impromptu tour, and now on the second floor, she wondered where Scout was. "Excuse me just a minute. I need to find my cat. I'll be right back."

Leaving Ava in the front master bedroom, Katherine began calling Scout. She checked two bedrooms, then headed to the back hallway. She thought she heard a woman sobbing. *What the hell. Who is that?*

As she rounded the corner and peered into the farthest bedroom, she spied an antique rocking chair, rocking back-and-forth, in a noisy, frantic fashion, but no one was sitting in it. Katherine felt an eerie, tingling feeling on the base of her neck. She started to back out of the room, but stopped when she heard a cat hissing.

Scout was crouched in the opposite corner. She'd arched her back and began lurching up and down like a deranged Halloween cat. Her eyes were glowing red, and fixed on the rocking chair.

Katherine moved toward her. "Scout, it's okay. We're leaving. Come to me."

The closed closet door popped open, and the sobbing continued inside.

Scout growled and then hissed. She slinked closer to the opening when Katherine grabbed her around the middle. "Oh, no, you don't."

Ava walked briskly into the room. "There you are. I see you found your cat, but why's her tail all bushed out?"

Katherine had to think of a good answer. She didn't want the realtor to know she and Scout had just encountered something very weird and unexplainable. "I think I startled her when I came into the room."

Scout collapsed against Katherine's chest. Her heart was beating fast. "Calm down, sweet girl. It's okay," she cooed to the frightened cat.

"Waugh," the Siamese cried.

Ava glanced around the room suspiciously, and didn't seem to buy Katherine's explanation.

Before Katherine could warn her not to, Ava walked over to the closet, pulled the light chain and looked inside. While she did that, Katherine held her breath for fear of what *was* inside.

Ava disappeared into the closet. "Wow, this is huge," she said. "Buyers love big closets."

Katherine cautiously stepped over and peeked inside. The closet was huge, almost the size of a small room.

Ava stepped out, and Katherine quickly closed the door.

Ava asked curiously. "If you don't mind my asking, who was the realtor this last time? I seem to remember it wasn't anyone local."

Katherine recovered, and walked out of the room. Scout was still afraid, and clung to her, breathing rapidly. "There have been several, but most recently the *List it Here* realty, in the city."

"Oh, yes. I've heard of them. Did they ever have an open house?"

"Not to my knowledge, they didn't."

"The house is very impressive. I'm surprised it hasn't sold."

Katherine thought, *Perhaps the sobbing woman in the closet turned off potential buyers.* "So, you've seen the house. Let's head back down. My cat has suddenly grown tired, and I must take her home," Katherine lied. Scout was a brave cat and rarely frightened by anything, but whatever the two of them had witnessed, it had scared the Siamese half-to-death. *There's no two ways about it,* Katherine thought. *Scout and I just had a paranormal experience.* She wanted to send Ava on her way, so she could research the house, make some inquiries, and call her spirit-hunting friend, Colleen.

Leaving the Foursquare and walking Ava to her car, Katherine said, "I really appreciate your offering to represent me in the sale of this house, but I'm not quite ready to list it again. Do you have a business card? I can call you when I'm ready."

"Yes, why of course," Ava said. She reached into her bag, and started to pull out a card. Before she handed it to Katherine, she said, "You know, these days, realtors don't have to bother sellers when showing their house. The owner puts the house key in a lock box, which hangs over the doorknob. When we need to get in, we simply punch in the combination, and extract the key."

"That's good to know," Katherine said, thinking it was a terrible idea, security-wise. She wondered how many people would know the combination, but kept her opinion to herself.

"Waugh!" Scout cried impatiently.

"Well, it's been nice meeting you," Ava said, handing Katherine her card. "Call me any time. Thanks so much for the tour. Enjoy the rest of your day."

"Nice meeting you, too," Katherine replied, watching the excessively eager realtor get in her car and pull away.

She whispered to Scout, "I'll carry you home. I was afraid, too. Something is off about that room. We need to find out what's going on."

"Ma-waugh," Scout agreed.

Katherine hurried back to the mansion, used her cell to enter a code to disarm the security alarm, and opened the door. Sitting inside the door, Abra wore an excited look, and acted like she'd been positioned there the entire time, waiting for Scout to get back home. Katherine gently put Scout down on the floor, unhooked the leash, and removed the cat harness. Scout bolted out of the entryway with Abra following. The two Siamese thundered upstairs and headed for the playroom in the turret bedroom.

Katherine walked into the living room and sat down on the floor. Sitting cross-legged, she didn't waste any time calling Colleen, who answered right away.

"Top of the mornin'," Colleen said with her slight Irish brogue.

"It's the afternoon, Carrot Top," Katherine joked. "Are you busy? I need to ask you a few things."

"I'm at the bungalow with Mum. Why don't you come over?"

"Oh, really? I didn't know you were coming to Erie today. Yes, I'll be right there."

Katherine grabbed her cross-over bag and left the mansion. She headed toward Alexander Street, where she owned a red brick bungalow — a genuine Sears Craftsman built in 1912. The house was too small for her growing cat family — now totaling seven, with Barbie Sanders' rehomed kittens — but the house was perfect for guests. Colleen's mum was staying there for a month to help Katherine with the wedding. Mum was like Katherine's second mom, especially since Katherine had lost her mother several years ago. Mum was going to have a part in the wedding: she was going to "give Katherine away."

Climbing the steps to the bungalow's front porch, Katherine didn't have time to ring the doorbell. Colleen opened the door, "Katz, hurry up and come in. I brewed some pumpkin spice tea, and Mum baked orange scones."

"That's what smells so delicious in here. At first, I thought you were burning one of those scented candles." The two headed to the kitchen.

"Hi, Mum," Katherine said, walking over and giving Mum a kiss on the cheek.

Mum was sitting at the built-in table, reading the Erie newspaper. "Hello, Katz. Grab a cuppa, and join us."

"I got it," Colleen said, reaching into a kitchen cabinet.

Katz slid onto the bench across from Mum. "Are you enjoying your stay?"

Colleen giggled, set down a cup and saucer in front of Katherine. "Mum's got a date tonight."

Katherine opened her mouth in surprise. "Really?" She wondered if it was Mum's guest on Cora's reception list.

Mum pursed her lips. "Not a date, Colleen. T'is merely dinner with a friend of Daryl's father."

Daryl was Colleen's boyfriend, and a deputy in the neighboring county. He was also Jake's cousin and was going to be the best man at the wedding.

Katherine thought, *Fast work, Mum. You've only been in town for a few days*, then said, "That's nice." She bit into a scone, which crumbled into pieces on the table. "Oops."

"I might have left something out," Mum pondered, absent-mindedly.

Colleen added, "Like vegetable oil?"

"I'm a bit daft. T'is a long time since I've had a date, I mean dinner, with a member of the opposite sex."

"What's his name? Where are you going?" Katherine asked.

"His name is James O'Ferrell, and he's taking me to the Erie Hotel's restaurant. His great grandparents were from Ireland, and immigrated to Indiana years ago to buy a farm."

Colleen added with an impish grin on her face, "Katz, he's filthy rich. He still works the family farm, but it's not a farm-farm with acres of corn, but a large, dairy farm."

Mum chimed in, "He's got a whole line of products from milk to ice cream to yogurt."

"For real?" Katherine asked. "What's the brand name?"

Colleen held up a pint of cream, sitting on the table. "A bit of cream for your tea?"

"Lady Moo Products," Katherine read the logo on the container. Katherine's face lit up, "Wow! I buy that brand at the Erie Market."

Colleen said to Katherine, "I know you didn't come over to talk about milk." Colleen and Katherine had been friends since grade school, and frequently read each other's thoughts.

Mum stood up. "I need to freshen up for *me* date. T'is grand to see ya, Katz."

"You, too! Have a wonderful time," Katherine said.

Colleen slid onto the bench opposite.

After Mum left the room, Katherine began, "You know that yellow brick house next door to me?"

"Yeah, the one that no one wants to buy," Colleen commented candidly.

"Scout and I just had something creepy happen to us at that house."

"What were you doing there? Shouldn't you be busy with your wedding stuff?"

"I know, but I got restless, and took Scout out for a walk with her new harness and leash. We ended up at the house."

"Okay, getting back to the house, since it was a speakeasy with gangsters and bootleggers, I'd suspect there'd be something off about it, like maybe it's haunted."

Colleen beamed enthusiastically. Spirit hunting was her area of expertise, because she once belonged to a ghost-hunting group in Manhattan.

Katherine shrugged. "I don't know. It's been on the market for over a year with no offers. Today while I was outside with Scout, a real estate lady approached me and asked to handle the listing. I took her on a tour."

Katherine recapped the haunting, complete with the rocking chair, Scout's reaction to the closet, and the invisible female voice.

Colleen's eyes grew big. "A chair rocking on its own —"

"The way it was moving, it looked like some invisible force was sitting in it, rocking away."

"Wait! Is the house furnished?"

"No, there isn't a stick of furniture except for that creepy chair."

"That's odd. Didn't Margie work on that house?"

"Yes, but she never mentioned anything that went bump in the night. I'll call her later."

"Okay, getting back to the facts, rocking chair symbolizes motherhood — a mom rocking her child. The mom is crying . . . but wait, are you sure it was an adult crying, or a child?"

"It was definitely an adult."

"Maybe the mom lost her child."

"Oh, how sad," Katherine frowned.

"Who lived there before?"

"I remember Mark Dunn said a woman named Mrs. Clay lived there for many, many years. She was a hoarder, and when she passed away, he had to make arrangements to empty the house."

"Maybe you should call him and ask if he ever felt anything odd in the house," Colleen suggested, "or knew of anyone else who did."

Katherine gave an amused look. "Surely you jest. Mark Dunn would think I'd gone mental. He'd be the last person I'd ask about the house."

"Do you think the Erie Library would have information about previous homeowners?"

"I was thinking more of the county courthouse. They would have property tax records. From there, I could get names of the people who lived there, and then go to the library. It's worth a trip."

"Good idea," Colleen said, then suggested. "How about I bring my spirit-hunting equipment, and we set up in the room?"

"Not liking that idea. It was scary enough the first time."

Colleen ignored the comment. "Is Friday night okay? I can't do it earlier, because I've got an exam coming up, and I need to study." Colleen was attending the same university in the city where Jake taught; she wanted to be a teacher.

"Great, but in the meantime, I plan on finding out as much as possible." Katherine got up. "Say 'bye' to Mum for me."

Katherine was halfway to the mansion when Margie, driving her pickup, pulled up alongside her. She lowered her window and said, "Hey, kiddo, it's a perfect day for a stroll in the park."

Katherine walked over to the driver's side, "Hi, Margie. How are you? How are the kids?"

"I'm doin' great, thank you. The kids are fine. Shelly got all As on her report card; Tommy did pretty good, but got a D in shop."

Katherine grimaced. "Maybe he didn't inherit Cokey's and your jack-of-all-trades genes."

Margie nodded, then said, "Or maybe he's too interested in the girls."

Katherine smiled. "Listen, I was over at the yellow brick house, and was surprised to see an old rocking chair in one of the bedrooms."

Margie tipped her head back and laughed. "Oh, my gosh. I forgot to haul that away. It was a joke with my drywall guys. They said it looked just like that rocking chair in the movie, *The Woman in Black*, with that actor that was in the Harry Potter movies. What's his name? Can't remember."

"Daniel Radcliffe. Did the guys ever sit in it?" Katherine joked, trying to mask a serious question.

"Have you forgotten? Those guys were the size of pro wrestlers. Not thinkin' they would have fit in it. Want me to move it today?"

"No, that's okay. I can leave it there until I put the house back on the market."

A truck pulled up behind Margie. Katherine waved him to go around. She had one more question to ask. "Did you ever encounter anything spooky in that house?"

Margie shook her head. "No, why?"

"Just asking. Sometimes these old houses give me the creeps."

"Nope, not this one. She's a happy house, and I'm surprised she hasn't sold. Well, kiddo, I was just headin' home to pick up some tools. Gotta get back to work."

"Talk to you soon," Katherine said, walking back to the sidewalk. *Happy house*, she thought. *Then why was the ghost crying?*

Chapter Five

Katherine opened the side door of the mansion and walked out. Earlier, she'd gotten a text message from Marcia, the daughter of her next door neighbor, Birdie Harper. Marcia was engaged to Evan Hamilton — a Vietnam veteran who was seriously disfigured in the war. He lived in secret in a cabin on the property that Katherine had bought a few months earlier. Marcia was stopping by for a visit.

Marcia drove up in her white Buick sedan and parked in front of the house. Katherine bounded down the concrete driveway to meet her.

"Hi, Marcia!" she called.

"Katz, hello! You will not *believe* my good news."

"What? Tell me?" Katherine said anxiously.

"I bought Evan a cell phone. Now when we're apart, we can send text messages to each other."

Katherine's cell pinged. She pulled it out of her jean's pocket. Evan had sent her a picture of his pet crow. Katherine giggled. She took a selfie of herself wearing a big grin. Evan texted back, "Morning sunshine!"

Katherine said to Marcia, "Come up on the porch, and 'have a sit down.'" She led the way.

Marcia laughed. "You really are becoming a Hoosier."

"Jake's an excellent coach."

Marcia joined her on the porch and sat on the swing. Katherine sat beside her.

Katherine returned Evan's text, "Marcia here. More later." She ended the message with a smiley face emoticon. She returned her cell to her pocket.

Marcia asked, "How are the wedding plans coming along?"

"Right at this very moment, Jake and Daryl are getting fitted for their tuxedos."

"I take it Daryl is the best man?"

Katherine nodded. "He's also Jake's cousin." Katherine switched the topic. "How are things at the cabin?"

"Pretty good," Marcia said slowly. She began to wring her hands, and judging by the grave look on her face, Katherine suspected she had something serious to say.

"What's wrong?"

"I'll just come right out with it," Marcia said uneasily. "Evan and I are moving."

"What?" Katherine said, shocked, with her mouth open. "Why? Did someone in the town find out about Evan's secret?"

"No, but it's only a matter of time. Evan doesn't want to be exposed."

"But he didn't concoct that 'haunting of Peace Lake' legend. His relatives did."

"Katz, confidentially, the legend is good for the town's economy. The romantic notion of a high school basketball legend dying in Vietnam and coming back to search for his lost love," Marcia stopped, and pointed at herself, "lost love being me . . . It appeals to tourists, making them want to visit the town."

"This is true, and when they visit, they also spend money at the local businesses."

Marcia sat up straight in the swing, turned and faced Katherine, "We don't want to start our married life under these circumstances."

Katherine put up her hand in the stop motion. "What? Married? When?" She smiled.

Marcia grinned. "Yes, dear, we are, but not in Indiana. After Evan gets his prosthetic eye, we're heading to New Mexico. Instead of buying property at Peace Lake and building there, as I intended, I've bought a house in a small town outside Santa Fe."

Recovering from shock, Katherine said, "Congratulations! I'm happy for the two of you. When are you moving?"

"We haven't decided yet, but we'll let you know." Marcia started to get up. "I've got a million errands to do before I drive back to the cabin. I'll keep in touch."

Katherine walked Marcia to her car, and waved as she drove away. She thought it was probably a good idea for Evan to leave Peace Lake. Who knows how many townspeople would be affected by the exposure of a bogus ghost story. Katherine knew in her heart that the couple needed to move where no one knew Evan's history. But she'd grown very fond of Evan, who treated her like a daughter. She brushed a tear from her cheek. She'd miss him terribly.

***

Jacky, Colleen's brother, and Katherine's long-time friend from Manhattan, drove erratically down the long driveway to the pink mansion, and nearly collided with a limestone column supporting the carport roof. A few minutes before, he'd texted Katherine and told her he'd arrived, rented a car from the Indy airport, and was now in town. He didn't tell her that he'd been in Erie for several hours, and been drinking a few pints at the Erie Hotel bar.

Stevie Sanders walked out of Mrs. Harper's back door, and headed to his truck. He fished a pack of cigarettes out of his canvas work shirt pocket, and lit one with a Bic lighter. Jacky nearly hit Stevie's truck when he parked. Stevie leaned against his tailgate and scowled.

Waiting outside the classroom door, Katherine observed Jacky's reckless driving, and also observed Stevie not being very happy. She worried that there might be an altercation; she hoped not.

Jacky, oblivious to how close he'd come to hitting Stevie's truck, got out of his rental car and ran over to Katherine. He picked her up and twirled her around, but instead of setting her back on the ground, he prolonged the hug. Katherine became uncomfortable, and pulled away.

"Did you make good time?" she asked.

"I have to say it was a bit turbulent, but the plane didn't crash." He winked, his green eyes narrowed in a flirtatious look.

Katherine smelled the liquor on his breath, and stepped back. "Do you want me to drive you to my guest house, so you can settle into your room before dinner?"

"I didn't know anything about a dinner."

"Oh, tonight Mum's throwing a dinner party in your honor. She's cooking lamb chops — your favorite. She's invited Daryl and Colleen, and Jake and me."

"I already told Mum I'm not stayin' with a bunch of noisy women. I rented me a room at the downtown hotel. I thought I'd get over here, so you wouldn't forget about me."

Katherine glanced uneasily over at Stevie, who continued leaning against his truck. He fished out a second cigarette, and lit it. She was becoming more uncomfortable standing next to Jacky, who was obviously intoxicated. She had serious reservations about inviting him inside.

It doesn't make any sense, she thought. *When Mum needed help with her drinking problem, Jacky was instrumental in getting her to a specialist. Yet here he is — drunker than a skunk.*

For want of something better to say, Katherine began, "You heard about my wrecking my SUV."

"I have to say I was a bit concerned." Jacky moved in fast and grabbed Katherine around the waist. He pulled her into a kiss.

Startled, Katherine struggled to move away. "Are you crazy? What are you doing?"

"I'm kissin' ya," Jacky said with a big grin on his face.

"Not happening," she said, her voice now loud with irritation. "I'm marrying Jake."

"Really?" he asked, with green eyes flashing. "Couples break up every day." He leaned in for another kiss.

Katherine retreated several feet. "Stop it, right now! I don't know what's gotten into you."

"It's simple, love. You're goin' dump that Indiana hillbilly, and marry me. I'm sick of waitin' in the wings."

Katherine was speechless, and then spoke, "Jacky, you are my friend — "

Jacky put up his right hand. "Stop preachin'. We were a couple until that Gary DeSutter bastard showed up. Look where that got ya?"

"Got me?" Katherine asked incredulously. "Gary dumped me for another woman, and then he was murdered in my house. Jacky, let me drive you back to the hotel."

Stevie came over and said to Jacky, "Hey, buddy, the lady doesn't want to talk to ya anymore, so you best git goin'." He had a tough expression on his face.

Jacky glared at Stevie, returning the menacing look. "Who the hell are you?"

"I'm a man who doesn't talk to a lady that way."

"You need to mind your own business."

Katherine intervened. "Jacky, you can't drive. Give me your keys?"

"Like hell," he said. "I'll walk to Mum's. Hey, Katz, where is it — your guest house?"

Katherine said with resignation, "I'll take you. I wanted to show you my new SUV anyway."

Stevie said, "Ma'am, you sure?"

"Thanks, Stevie, but I'm good."

Stevie walked back to his truck and watched until Katherine and Jacky drove away.

Chapter Six

The next day, Katherine climbed in her black Subaru Outback and drove to the Erie County Courthouse on the edge of town. She passed the Red House Diner, and snickered at the crowded parking lot full of pickup trucks. Clearly, it was the town's gossip hour.

She angled into a parking space in front of the courthouse, which stood like a giant, stone edifice — two stories of hand-hewn limestone, quarried from a neighboring county. Tall, arched windows broke up the coldness of the building. Katherine thought it needed stone gargoyles, standing guard from the top of four newel posts that formed the Widow's Walk. The large clock on the front tower's face sounded two loud bongs.

Katherine whisked through a revolving door and made her way to the information desk. A tall, regal-looking man dressed very formally in a business suit, wearing wire-rim glasses, asked her if she needed any help.

"Hello, I'm Katherine Kendall," she introduced.

The man stifled a laugh. "I'm Jake's great-uncle, Alan." He extended his hand.

Katherine shook it, and said, "Nice meeting you. I'm discovering that Jake has a very *large* family."

"Yes, indeed. Congratulations are in order. Jake makes us very proud."

"Thank you," she glowed.

"So, what brings you here today?"

"I own the house next to the pink mansion. I mean, let me start all over again. I inherited the pink mansion from my great-aunt Orvenia Colfax. I also inherited the yellow brick Foursquare next to it."

"The speakeasy," Alan teased.

"You've heard of it?"

"It's an Erie landmark, except it's not on the historic register."

"I'm looking for information about the history of its previous owners."

"That shouldn't be hard to find, but let me get someone to relieve me here. I'll take you back to the Recorders Office." Alan lifted a landline receiver and called someone to the front. In a few seconds, a middle-aged woman sauntered out of an office and said, "I'll take over now." She eyed Katherine curiously, but didn't smile. Katherine smiled anyway. She had long gotten used to the town's cliques. If you didn't belong to one, you were regarded an outsider. And never talk bad about anyone in town, because everyone was related either by kin or on-going friendships.

Alan said, "Thanks, Marty. Katherine, I'll show you the way."

Katherine followed him down to the last room, and entered the Recorders Office.

"Please, take a seat," he pointed. He went into a vault-like room, and returned with a large binder. He studied the index, then turned to a page. "The house was built in 1920. The owner was William Colfax."

Katherine sat down on an oak side chair, then nodded. She already knew this information.

"When William passed away, legal title went to Orvenia Colfax."

"Yes, my great-aunt. Does the record indicate the names of tenants? I mean, if William or my great-aunt rented the home to a tenant, would their names appear in the record?"

"No, only the names of the owners. Why would you want the names of the renters?" Alan asked nosily.

Katherine got up, and answered evasively. "I'm curious like a cat."

"Evelyn Clay lived there for decades."

"Do you know if she was married?"

"She married Ron Clay. He was a friend of my dad. They were on the same bowling team. The couple didn't get along. Ron was socially active, but Evelyn just wanted to stay in the house. She was a recluse."

Katherine added, "When I first moved here, and she was still alive, I never saw her, not even to check the mail or walk in her backyard."

"Ron couldn't find work in Erie, so he took a coal mining job in southern Indiana. He died tragically in a mining accident."

Katherine wondered if the spirit was Ron Clay. "I'm sorry to hear that. Do you know if they had any children?"

"They had a daughter," he paused. "Let me think for a minute, and I'll try to remember her name. What was it?" he said, pulling at his white goatee.

"That would be so helpful," Katherine encouraged.

"Started with a 'K.' Kathy, no, not Kathy. Katrina. Katrina Clay. That was her name."

"Does she still live in Erie?"

"Let me think," he pondered. "I remember there was some gossip in town about Katrina falling for some farmhand. Evelyn didn't like the young man, so she sent Katrina to a finishing school in Massachusetts."

"Wow, that seems rather extreme. What did Katrina's father think of that?"

"Oh, he was dead by then."

"What was the year Katrina was sent away?"

"Sometime during the mid-1960s, don't rightly remember."

"Do you know if Katrina ever returned to Erie?"

Alan shook his head. "I don't know. After a while people stopped talking about her, and the young man went his separate way. Ms. Kendall, Katrina would be in her seventies now. You might want to check the state's death record database."

"Thanks for the tip."

"My pleasure. Here, I'll write down the web address. You can search online."

"I appreciate it," Katherine said, and then thought about how she was a computer science expert, and should have thought of searching online in the first place. But she prided herself in getting out and meeting new people. She didn't want to become a recluse like Evelyn Clay.

Alan scribbled the address on a memo pad, tore off the sheet, and handed it to her. "Let me know what you find out. You've piqued my interest. I like to know what happened to her."

"Will do. Thanks so much," she said, heading for the door. "It's been nice talking to you, Alan. I hope to see you soon."

Alan called after her. "You will! Me and the Mrs. are coming to your reception at the armory."

"Wonderful. I look forward to meeting her. Bye, now."

***

Katherine drove home, and immediately walked back to her office, and woke up the computer. Keying in the Internet address Alan had given her, she waited for the prompt, then typed in Katrina Clay's name, filled in the town name, and pressed "Enter." Five Katrina Clays popped up on screen, but none of them was from Erie.

"That was a bust," she said out loud. "Why even ask for the town name, when you're going to list all the Katrinas in the state?" She suddenly realized she had become one of those individuals who talked to computers. "Whoa. I get it. Maybe one of the five is my Katrina, but she died somewhere else in Indiana." She painstakingly went through each name; none of them matched the time

79

frame. The women were either too young or too old when they died. "Enough! I'm done."

Swiveling in her chair, she became aware she hadn't been greeted by the cats. "Lucky seven, where are you?" she beckoned, thinking they were probably upstairs taking a siesta in their playroom. The kittens, Dewie and Crowie, raced into the room, and applied their paw brakes close to Katherine's chair. She reached down, picked up both of them, and placed them on her lap. "Want me to teach you how to surf the web?" she asked playfully.

"Mao," Dewie belted; Crowie patted the mouse.

Surprised, Katherine said, "Looks like you've already had lessons. Okay, now off you go." She set the kittens on the floor. They scampered out of the room, and into the atrium.

Katherine began searching the *Erie Ledger* for possible articles on either Katrina Clay or the yellow brick house. She plugged in the address, and meticulously combed through article after article, based on the year. She was thankful that she'd made funds available to the Erie library to enter the digital age, or else she'd be in the library right now, searching through microfilm with an ancient reader that belonged in the Smithsonian. After an hour of reading about the local cake bake, church trips to northern Indiana, and fatal car crashes, obviously before seat belts, she changed gears and searched for obituaries.

"Bingo," she said out loud. "December 23, 1940, twenty-year-old Rita Booker, domestic worker for the Colfax family, was hit by a car on Lincoln Street. She died later as a result of the accident."

Where on Lincoln Street? Katherine asked herself. "Was she married? Was she a mom? She continued reading. "Funeral at the Erie Church of God, interment in the Ethel cemetery after short service."

Frustrated, Katherine sent the information to the printer. Then she exited the site, pulled up an advanced search window in her browser, and rekeyed the database address Alan Cokenberger had provided. Scanning the page, she read Rita's death certificate. She gasped, "She was pregnant."

With fingers flying, she texted Colleen. "Drum roll! The ghost is . . . ."

Colleen texted back, "Spirit." Colleen constantly reminded her that the politically correct word for ghost was spirit. "Man or woman?"

"A young woman who worked for my great-aunt."

"What year?"

"1940."

"Cool, see ya tonight."

Wow, that was abrupt, Katherine thought, then remembered that today was Colleen's exam day. "I hope I didn't jinx it."

***

Katherine sat on the top step of the yellow brick Foursquare and waited for Daryl and Colleen to arrive. In a few minutes, the couple pulled up in Daryl's classic 1967 Impala. The off-duty deputy got out and moved over to open Colleen's door. The door made a loud creak when he opened it. Colleen slid out, and opened the back passenger door. Katherine got up from the step and walked down the sidewalk to meet them. "Hi, you two."

Daryl smiled. "How ya doin', Katz?"

Colleen lifted a cardboard box off the back seat. Daryl walked over, and took the box. "Here, let me help you with that."

Katherine said, "I'm just fine. Are you sure you don't want to join us in our paranormal investigation?"

Daryl moved toward the Foursquare. "Normally, I'd be all over it, but Jake and I have plans."

Katherine knew what those plans were. Tonight was the bachelor party. Jake's friends and cousins had reserved a dining room at the Erie Hotel. She smiled, "I know."

Colleen said, "Katz, I didn't bring all of my equipment, but just the most important ones."

Daryl, always the deputy, even when he was off-duty, said, "Katz, can I do a look-see inside the house before you two start your séance?"

Colleen threw him an annoyed look. "We're not having a séance."

Daryl winked affectionately, and put his hands up in defense. "I'm just messin' with you."

Colleen pursed her lips.

"Sure, Daryl, I just unlocked the door. Colleen and I will wait outside," Katherine answered.

"Does anyone else have keys?" he asked.

"Margie has a set. Plus, Jake. Why?"

"Does Margie know you two are," he paused, to say the correct terminology in front of Colleen, "investigating paranormal activity?"

Colleen smiled. "That's better."

"No. What are you getting at? Do you think Margie's lurking inside waiting to pretend to be a ghost?" Katherine laughed.

"Just askin'." Daryl opened the front door, and stepped inside. Colleen moved over to the top step, and sat down.

"Hey, Colleen. What gives? You look a bit glum."

"I'm fine," Colleen said, not very convincingly.

"No, you're not. What gives?"

"I'm having problems with Daryl."

"Really?" Katherine asked, surprised.

"Do not breathe a word of this to Jake. Promise?"

"Of course. What's wrong?"

85

"Daryl is pressuring me to get married, and I don't want to. I just started school — "

"You think he's moving too fast?"

Colleen nodded.

Daryl returned. "Coast is clear. Ladies, I better be goin'." He kissed Colleen on the cheek, and headed for his car.

Katherine waved and ushered Colleen in. "I think he adores you."

"I've got you figured out, Katz. You just want me to tell you I'm madly in love with Daryl."

"Well? Are you?"

"Don't jinx it. Surely you haven't forgotten my last relationship disaster with Mario."

"I think you're safe with Daryl. I know as a matter of fact he won't be moving to Italy."

"Okay, where's the room?" Colleen asked abruptly, stooping down to pick up the box in the foyer, where Daryl had put it.

"This way," Katherine said, heading for the stairs. She turned right at the landing, and walked down the hallway to the back bedroom. Earlier, Jake had carried the haunted rocking chair to the basement, then, back in the bedroom, he set up two folding chairs. Colleen positioned her box on one of them.

Katherine said lightly, "I'm so glad that horrible rocking chair isn't in here."

Frigid air rushed into the room, and the heavy door to the room slammed shut, with such force that Katherine thought the door frame would collapse.

Two more doors shut loudly in the hallway, and then there was an eerie calm.

Colleen said, eyes wide open, "Katz, remember what our mums used to tell us before we went to school. Need I refresh your memory?"

"Okay!" Katherine said defensively. "I'll mind my manners."

"T'wasn't kind of you to show disrespect."

Katherine looked at Colleen like her Irish friend had lost her mind, and mouthed the words, "What do I say now?"

Colleen whispered, "Apologize."

Katherine didn't know where to look, up, down, or sideways, so she gazed at the closed door. She'd never apologized to an unseen spirit, but she put her best foot forward. "I am so sorry. I didn't mean to insult your rocking chair."

There was a dead silence, then the closet door creaked opened a few inches.

Katherine wanted to bolt from the room, but forced herself to sit down, instead. After a few seconds, Colleen resumed taking items out of her box. "Can I help with anything?" Katherine asked, still a little shaken.

"I'm good," Colleen answered, removing a K2 EMF meter, a mini-Maglite flashlight, a small metal wind chime, candles, and an old-fashioned, mercury house thermometer.

"The only high tech gizmo I see is the ghost meter. Why the other stuff?"

"Spirit," Colleen reminded. She moved over to the windowsill of the right window. Removing the strap of her shoulder-bag, she placed the purse on the sill. She drew out a plastic hook, and peeled off the plastic backing. She pressed the hook on the underside of the top window frame, then hung the wind chime. She explained, "My paranormal group uses the wind chime to monitor changes in the atmosphere, which may indicate a spirit."

Katherine said under her breath, "Why bother? We've already encountered it."

"I'm trying to be objective here," Colleen said in a serious tone. She took the house thermometer and placed it on the sill. "Please note it's sixty-eight degrees in here now. The mercury thermometer works better than the modern digital ones. They're more sensitive to temperature changes —"

"Why is that?" Katherine interrupted.

"It could interfere with the K2 meter, which measures spikes in electromagnetic energy. Oh, before I forget, hand over your cell phone."

"Why?"

"Because it could also interfere with the K2."

"Couldn't I just put it into airplane mode?"

"Not so much."

"Okay," Katherine said reluctantly. Extracting her cell from her cross-over bag, she powered it down. Colleen removed her cell as well, and started to walk to the bedroom door.

Katherine said quickly. "Where are you going?"

"I'm going to take the phones to the front bedroom, and shut the door."

"You can't go out there alone," Katherine said, getting up.

Colleen opened the door a crack and looked out. "I'll be back in a minute," she said, stepping out.

Katherine walked right behind her.

"What are you doing?" Colleen asked.

"I've seen too many scary movies. When someone says they'll be right back, that means in two seconds flat the bogeyman gets them."

"Okay, whatever. Come with me."

They both walked to the front bedroom, glancing side-to-side in case something went bump in the night. Colleen placed both phones in a closet and shut the door. When they returned to the back hall bedroom, they were startled to see the wind chime lying in the middle of the floor.

"Colleen, I think we should go home," Katherine said, frightened. "This place gives me the creeps."

"Please, Katz, I haven't even started yet. Can we stay until I say *when*?"

Katherine didn't answer right away, hesitated, and said in a low voice, "I guess so."

"I'll take that as a 'yes.'" Colleen took three candles with glass holders out of the box, placed two on the windowsill, and one in the corner, on the floor. She lit each one with a long-barreled candle lighter. The candlelight bathed the room in a warm glow as the sun set. Colleen explained, "There's another reason why I always take candles. I've been in several haunted houses where midway through the investigation, the electricity goes out."

"Well, Carrot Top, that's good to know, because if the power goes off, you'll be the first to see the back of me flying out the door."

Colleen gave Katherine a warning look. "Katz, promise me, whatever happens, you don't flip out and trip over the candle. My mission this evening is to *not* set the house on fire."

"Hear! Hear!" Katherine agreed. "But could we at least have the overhead light on?"

Colleen walked over to the wall light switch, and flipped it on. The single bulb in the ceiling light fixture burned out immediately.

"Did you see that?" Katherine asked, surprised.

"Do you have any replacement bulbs in the house?"

"Not that I'm aware of. Okay, so no ceiling light. Switch the light on in the closet. It's a chain hanging down." Katherine remembered Scout's frightened reaction when the closet door opened by itself.

Colleen didn't move. Katherine didn't either.

Katherine was the first to speak, "Double dog dare you."

"Okay, fine. Whatever," Colleen said, cautiously stepping over to the closet, opening the door, and yanking the light chain. The bulb illuminated the spacious closet, but barely lit the bedroom. "I should have brought more candles."

Colleen removed the last item from the box — a blue, mini-Maglite flashlight. She took it over to the left window and placed it on the sill. "Okay, Katz, I'll do the speaking from here on out. Please be calm, and open up your mind to explore the unknown."

Katherine took out a folded piece of paper from her pocket. "Here's the list of questions I want you to ask."

"Sure, fine," Colleen said, taking it. She studied it, then put it in her pocket.

Colleen set the cardboard box on the floor behind her chair, and sat down. She placed the K2 meter on the floor in front of her. "Remember Katz, the meter, right now, shows green. If a spirit is detected, the needle will shoot to red."

"Yes, I remember."

Colleen was quiet for a moment, then said, "Hello. My name is Colleen Murphy, and this is my friend, Katherine Kendall. Her nickname is Katz. We want to communicate with you this evening. We are not here to harm you in any way. We just want to ask you a few questions."

Colleen got up and moved to the flashlight. She picked it up off the window sill. "This flashlight easily twists on and off." Colleen demonstrated how to do so.

"I'm going to leave it off. When you want to answer "yes" to my question, you can twist it on for a moment, then twist it off, and wait until my next question. If the answer is no, please do not twist the flashlight. I will wait thirty seconds before I ask you the next question." Colleen set the flashlight back on the sill, and sat back down.

"Katz and I know you are here, and want to communicate with you. Are you a man?"

Katz turned in her seat, and looked over her shoulder at the flashlight.

"I'll ask again. If you are a man, will you please turn on the flashlight?"

Katherine whispered, "I don't think it's a man."

Colleen looked at her watch. When thirty seconds had gone by, she continued, "Okay, if you are a woman, would . . . ?"

The flashlight flashed on, and then in a few seconds, turned back off.

"Thank you," Colleen said. "I know what you just did takes a lot of energy, and I respect that. If you are Evelyn Clay, would you turn the flashlight on?"

The flashlight remained off.

"If you are not Evelyn Clay, are you Rita Booker? Did you die in 1940 outside this house?"

Katherine was on the edge of her seat. A draft of cold air chilled her to the bone. She looked at Colleen to see if she'd felt it, too. Colleen nodded and pointed to the thermometer, which now read fifty degrees. The needle on the K2 was in the red zone.

The flashlight didn't turn on. They waited a minute, then Colleen asked, "Are you a mom?"

The flashlight vibrated lightly on the windowsill, flickered on, and then off.

"Are you expecting a child?"

The wind chime tinkled slightly, and the candle flames splattered. The flashlight shot off the windowsill, and bounced on the floor, skidding to a halt against the closet's wall, then the closet door slammed with great force. They could hear a woman sobbing on the other side of the door.

Katherine jumped in her seat. "That's what Scout and I heard. Okay, Colleen, I don't think she wants to talk to us anymore. Can we go now?"

Colleen put up her finger, and whispered, "Just one second," then addressed the spirit. "We are sorry we upset you. We are leaving now, and will check on you another time."

Katherine said, "Oh, no we won't." She grabbed her cross-over bag off the chair, and headed for the door. Colleen said haughtily, "Well, at least help me gather up my stuff."

Katherine grabbed the box, and the two started loading equipment into it. On the way out of the house, Katherine shut off the first floor lights. Colleen had already left, and was waiting on the porch. Something caught the corner of Katherine's eye.

Katherine glanced at the stairwell. A blurry, translucent shape glided down the steps. Her hair was shoulder-length, and flipped up at the ends. She wore a madras blouse with a pair of green shorts. Her knee socks matched the shorts; on her feet were penny loafers. Katherine thought she looked like a teenager from the 1960s, because the blouse was like one her mom wore in an old photo from that decade. The apparition was sobbing. She clutched in her hand a baby blanket.

Katherine didn't hesitate to run. She sprinted to the front door, then looked back. The apparition was gone. She hurriedly shut the door and nervously fumbled for the key in her pocket. She locked the door, and joined Colleen on the porch.

Colleen asked, "Are you okay? What just happened in there?"

"I saw a ghost."

"Shut the door! I wanna see. Let's go back."

"Ah, no. Let the dead rest."

Colleen snickered, "I can't believe you said that. The poor woman is anything but at rest."

"Try teenaged girl. Our sobbing spirit probably isn't over thirteen-years-old."

Colleen said excitedly. "We have more research to do."

"Oh, and Colleen, most importantly, we've got to move that rocking chair back upstairs."

"Brilliant," Colleen retorted. "Let's go get it right now — "

"I'm getting married tomorrow, and I'm exhausted. How about I take a raincheck until after the honeymoon?"

"I know. Are you the least bit nervous?"

"About a spirit? Well — "

"No, don't be daft, about getting married."

"Honestly, I wish Jake and I had run off to Vegas months ago, but if we did, I'm sure Cora would insist on a reception anyway."

"Are you sure you don't want a drink at the Erie Hotel?"

"Carrot Top, it's bad luck to see your future husband the night before."

"What? Let's get our superstitions straight. It's bad luck for the groom to see the bride in her gown before the wedding."

"Whatever. I'll drive you home," Katherine yawned.

"Can you drop me off at the bungalow? I'm staying with Mum tonight."

"Sure, I'll go get the car."

"I'll come with you. I don't want the bogeyman to get you." Colleen tipped her head back and laughed.

Chapter Seven

Katherine, Colleen, and Mum were upstairs in the front bedroom of the pink mansion. Katherine was fussing with her dress, which was a knee-length, layered, lace dress with a square neckline and silver beaded bodice. Tugging at the waist, she said, "Women back in the day must have been super tiny."

Colleen commented, "Your great-aunt must have been a size zero. Do you think this was her wedding dress?"

Katherine shrugged. "I don't know, but I found it in her vintage clothing collection. The new museum curator let me borrow it."

Mum said happily. "Katz, you look absolutely stunning. Your great-aunt, in heaven, must be smilin' down upon you."

Katherine's eyes grew big. "Oh, no," she said, surprised.

"What's the matter?" Mum asked.

"I think the lining just ripped."

"Get out!" Colleen said. "Quick, Katz. Where's your sewing kit?"

"I'll get it," Katherine said, moving for the door.

Mum said, "No, don't move. Take the dress off."

Katherine said to Colleen, "In the back guest room, in the tall dresser, there's a sewing kit. I think it's in the second drawer."

"Got it," Colleen said, rushing out of the room.

Katherine carefully took off the white dress and handed it to Mum. Mum reached into her purse, drew out her reading glasses, and put them on. She gently turned the dress inside out and scrutinized the lining. "It's a small tear. I can mend it."

"I shouldn't have eaten so much food Thursday night," Katherine said, remembering the giant prime rib and baked potato covered with sour cream and butter. Jake's mother had organized a rehearsal dinner at the Erie Hotel.

Colleen returned with the sewing kit. Mum grabbed the box and opened it. She hurriedly threaded a needle and began stitching the tear.

Colleen said anxiously. "Mum, hurry up. We've got five minutes."

"Hold your tongue, Missy. I'm sewin' as fast as I can," Mum scolded.

Judge Hartman, the wedding officiant, knocked on the door.

"Hello, Judge," Katherine said. "Come in."

"Hello, ladies. Oh, my goodness, what happened?" she asked Katherine, who was standing in the middle of the room wearing a slip.

Katherine answered. "Slight setback. We may need a few extra minutes. Have all the guests arrived?"

The judge was privy to the guest list, which numbered fewer than twenty.

"Yes," the judge smiled. "Cokey, Margie, and their daughter just arrived. They were escorting Jake's grandparents to the atrium when I came up to check on you. Jake's parents, Johnny and Cora are here. Daryl's folks, too. Linda Martin and Mark Dunn came first. I forget the name of the kid in charge of the music."

Katherine giggled, "That's Cokey's and Margie's son, Tommy. He's a twelve-year-old musical wonder."

"Russell's already snapping pictures," the judge said, beaming.

Katherine knew the couple had been dating, but she also knew Russell had asked Elsa out for a date after the reception. Elsa declined because she was taking care of the cats, but agreed to meet him for drinks after Jake and she returned from the honeymoon. She didn't think the judge would be beaming if she knew that bit of info, but her lips were sealed. She thought, *Please, dear God, no drama on my wedding day.*

"'Tis fixed," Mum announced, using her teeth to cut the thread.

The judge said, "Ladies, I'll head downstairs. Katz, I know we rehearsed this Thursday night, but can you refresh my memory on how you'll give me the signal to begin?"

"I'll text you, but promise me, you'll turn off your phone after you've read it."

"Will do," the judge said, leaving.

"Oh, could you please find Elsa and ask her to come up?" Katherine asked.

"Yes, of course," the judge answered.

Mum warned, "Katz, the lace is a bit fragile on this dress, but if anythin', the beads and the love of Mary will be holdin' it together."

Colleen frowned, "That's encouraging, Mum," then to Katherine, "I'm glad you didn't put me in one of those three-million-year-old dresses." Colleen wore a mid-sleeved, V-neck short dress in emerald green. It complemented her long, red hair.

Katherine smiled, took the mended wedding dress from Mum, and pulled it over her head. She sighed.

"I heard that," Colleen said. "What's up?"

"I wish my Mom and Dad were here."

Mum walked over and hugged Katherine. "'Tis okay. They're here in spirit, I tell ya. Don't fret on your weddin' day."

Katherine fought back the tears and said, "Colleen, help me with this foreband. I'll hold the front, if you attach the back."

"Here, give it to me. I think it'll work better if I simply clasp it first . . . ." Colleen took the Swarovski crystal foreband and placed it over Katherine's short black hair, which had been swept back from her face. Katherine looked approvingly in the mirror. "Okay, that about wraps things up."

Mum said, "Where's your earrings?"

"Oh, I almost forgot." Katherine moved to the dresser and opened a small cloisonné box. Taking out a pair of emerald and diamond earrings, she said, "These were my Mom's."

Both Mum and Colleen admired the earrings. Mum reached in her purse and pulled out a Tiffany blue jewelry pouch. She handed it to Katherine. "I want you to have this. It's a little something I found in Manhattan for you to wear for good luck."

Katherine opened the pouch to find a sterling silver Claddagh pendant with a deep blue gem. "Mum," she gushed. "It's beautiful."

"It's your birthstone. The jeweler said it's Tanzanite."

"Help me put it on."

Mum got up and took the necklace from Katherine. She pinched the lobster claw and wound the necklace around Katherine's neck. "The necklace accomplishes two things at the same time: it's new and blue."

Colleen moved over. Taking her cell phone out of her bag, she snapped several pictures.

Elsa came in wearing a very low-neck, sexy, black cocktail dress, with high-heeled sandals. "Wow, Katz, you look like you just jumped off the cover of *Glamour* magazine."

Katherine radiated. "Thank you, and so do you."

Since August, Elsa had been Katz's official cat-wrangler. Her job was to mind the cats while Jake and Katherine attended their wedding reception, and afterward take care of the felines for a few days while the couple was away. She was also in charge of getting Scout and Abra ready for their part in the wedding ceremony. Elsa held up a handled bag from a specialty pet accessories store. "I've got the cats' collars, and Abra's cape."

"I can't wait to see them," Katherine said enthusiastically.

Elsa extracted two blue, rhinestone-studded collars wrapped in pink tissue paper. The lace cape was edged with amethyst-colored rhinestones.

Colleen asked, "Why's there only one cape?"

Katherine smirked. "Because we can't get a cape on Scout, but we can on Abra."

Elsa giggled. "Katz, I hope you don't mind, but I got these charms for their collars." She held one of them up.

Katherine leaned in closer to take a look. "It's a silver cat charm. How cute."

"It's sterling silver so it'll never tarnish. It fits perfectly on the collar's metal D-ring thingy. Scout's neck is a tad bigger than Abra's, so to tell the collars apart, I'll put the single cat charm on Scout's, and the charm with two cats on Abra's. That way we won't get them mixed up."

"Adorable," Katherine said. "Thanks so much. It was very sweet of you."

"My pleasure," Elsa said, inching to the door. "Okay, before I leave, let me quickly go over my part. After you go downstairs, I'll wait up here by the landing. When I hear the famous words, 'with this ring,' I'll send Abra down first. But, right now, I want to go to the playroom, and put the collars on Scout and Abra. Then I'll hang out with the cats. Can you knock when you're going down?"

"Yes. Oh, and please, make sure they're locked in the playroom with the other cats when the ceremony is finished."

"Of course, no problem. Actually, Katz, I have Scout's and Abra's new cat carrier tucked away downstairs in the living room. As soon as their part is finished, I'll put them in it. I'll wait until the service is over, then I'll carry them upstairs. See ya later," Elsa said, leaving the room.

Katherine meant to call after her, and say that putting Scout and Abra in the carrier wasn't a good idea, but she got distracted by Mum. Scout hated the carrier and would be quite vocal in letting the wedding guests know.

"Katz, love, I'm going downstairs," Mum said. "I'll meet you at the bottom landing, as rehearsed. Oh, and Colleen, with those spikey heels, hang on to the handrail. Be careful coming down."

Colleen rolled her eyes, "Yes, Mum."

After Mum left, Katherine said to Colleen. "I'm a nervous wreck, but when I see Jake, I'll know that everything will be okay."

Colleen pinched her on the arm, "Aren't you glad you moved out here to find the perfect man?"

Katherine grinned ear-to-ear. She grabbed her beaded purse and extracted her cell phone. She sent a text to the judge to begin. Also, she asked her to signal Tommy to begin the Wedding March. Muting her phone, she took Colleen by the arm. "Age before beauty," she joked.

Colleen tossed back her hair and quipped, "We're two months apart. And, Miss Katz, you're older."

The sound of the cats in the playroom had become very loud. Katherine wondered if Elsa had them playing with the laser pointer toy.

Colleen whispered, "Shouldn't Elsa be trying to calm them down, instead of getting them all riled up?"

"I'll poke my head in, and see what's going on." Katherine slowly opened the door, and tried to peek in. Iris squeezed through the tiny opening, and bolted down the stairs. Katherine hastened after her. Iris stopped abruptly on the second landing.

Katherine called, "Come here, Miss Siam." Iris craned her neck, and tried to push her head through the balusters. Taking one look at the gathering, she hissed, and hiked it back upstairs. Katherine grabbed her and held her close. She whispered, "I promise to check on you later." Katherine could hear loud laughter from the guests below. "Wish me luck, my treasures," she said to her cats.

Iris yowled, Abby chirped, and Lilac me-yowled. Abra cried a sweet "raw." But Scout cried a loud "waugh," which seem to say to the other cats, "Shut up already, and move away from the door."

"Thanks, Scout. I'll see you in a minute," Katherine said, closing the door.

"Wait," Elsa said, following after her. "I'm sorry. I promise not to open the door until I hear the word. I'll stay right here."

After the laughter died down, Tommy fired up the CD player, and the Wedding March began — again.

Colleen said, "Let's get this show on the road." She descended two steps and nearly tripped. Looking back at Katz, she said, "I meant to do that."

Katherine waited until Colleen had gone down the second landing, then slowly made her descent. When she turned the corner, all she could see was Jake — the love of her life — waiting for her. Her brown-haired, brown-eyed handsome man looked dashing in his tuxedo. She never felt so happy.

The feeling was mutual. Jake's adoring eyes locked onto hers.

Mum met her at the foot of the stairs and took her hand. She led Katherine over to where Jake was standing. Katherine scanned the room and smiled at each of the guests. Grandpa Cokenberger blew her a kiss while Grandma nudged him in the ribs.

Judge Hartman stood in parlor doorway, behind a podium. She nodded at Tommy to stop the music, which he did without a hitch. She said to the small audience, "Who presents this woman to be married to this man?"

Mum answered in her Irish brogue, "On behalf of those who are with us, and those who have gone before, I give my blessin' to this union." She placed Katherine's hand in Jake's.

The couple stepped closer to the podium, with best man, Daryl, and maid of honor, Colleen, flanked on Jake's and Katherine's sides.

"Katherine Orvenia Kendall, do you take Jake Johnny Cokenberger as your lawfully wedded husband?"

"I do," Katherine said, glowing.

"Jake, do you take Katherine to be your legal wedded wife, to have and to hold from this day forward?"

"I do," Jake leaned in and kissed Katherine on the cheek.

Smiling at the ab lib, Katherine winked. Jake continued, "Katz, before these witnesses, I vow to love you and care for you for as long as we both shall live."

A happy tear slid down Katherine's cheek and she squeezed his hand.

The judge continued, "The exchange of wedding rings represent the vows and promises the bride and groom have exchanged."

Hearing the cue, Elsa opened the playroom door, and was startled to see Scout and Abra curled together on top of one of the cat trees — fast asleep. Abra was snoring.

"Scout! Abra!" Elsa called. "Wake up! Why did you go to sleep?"

Scout raised her head and muttered a mild protest. Her sapphire-blue eyes were crossed, and one fang showed.

"Hurry up, you two," Elsa pleaded. "They're waiting downstairs."

The Siamese casually jumped down. Meanwhile, the other cats were waking up too. Iris had already made a beeline for the door. Lilac and Abby were running to the door, as well.

"Oh, no you don't. Get back. Back!"

Elsa was too late. Iris escaped and streaked down the stairs. She could hear raucous laughter from below. "Oh, great, some cat sitter I am," she said out loud. Shutting the door, she planned her next strategy.

Inside, Scout and Abra were taking their sweet time coming to the door. Meanwhile, Lilac and Abby vowed to get out, as well.

Elsa slowly opened the door again just enough to wedge her right foot in. Maybe the threat of a mild shoe-nudge would stop the feline escape. Lilac jumped over her foot, while Abby hunkered down and slittered under it. Both shot down the stairs.

Elsa glanced irritably at the seal-point sisters. "Both of you are such brats. Hope you're having fun annoying me."

"Ma-waugh," Scout agreed, then slowly slinked out of the room, muttering a volley of Siamese. Once outside the playroom, Scout yawned while Abra stretched.

Elsa looked up at the ceiling, in frustration. She stooped down, grabbed Abra, and attached the wedding cape to the cat's collar. She tugged the jeweler's ring box from her dress pocket and placed it on the floor. Scout inched toward it.

"No, not you," Elsa cautioned. "You've already got Katz's ring for Jake on your collar. This is for Abra."

The rehearsed plan was for Abra to trot down the stairs first with Scout following a minute later. They had practiced the routine many times, and each time the Siamese had nailed it — without any catly deviations from the plan. Until . . .

"Abra, are you ready?" Elsa whispered.

Jake called again, "Abra, bring it."

Abra grasped the box with her V-shaped jaws. She sprinted down the steps, four-at-a-time, with such speed her cape blew backward, like Superman's. Scout ran behind her.

Elsa, freaking out, said, "Scout, come back here. You're not supposed to go yet."

Scout stopped on the first landing and sassed a loud "waugh," which seemed to say to Elsa, "Go to blazes. I'll go when I want to go."

Elsa threw up her hands, and said, "I give up!" She carefully walked down the stairs in her high-heeled sandals. Stopping on the bottom step, she studied the room. She spotted Iris peeking out from behind the Eastlake hall tree, but Lilac and Abby were nowhere to be seen. And Scout and Abra were missing, too. Elsa was relieved that none of the wedding guests noticed her, and that all eyes were on the happy couple.

Jake said again, "Abra, bring it to me."

Abra came out from underneath the chair Grandpa Cokenberger was sitting on. When Grandpa felt her brush by his leg, he broke into a loud laugh. "Here, kitty, kitty."

Abra gave a side glance of extreme distaste to the elderly man. She didn't like being called "kitty." She was a Siamese diva, and expected to be addressed that way.

The guests cooed and awed at the sight of Abra in her lace cape. Still clutching the jeweler's box in her jaws, she approached Jake, rubbing the side of her face against his leg. Abra was in her element, loving every second of attention until the judge's cell phone rang an annoying Sci-fi themed ringtone.

"Oh, no," Katherine whispered to Jake, recalling the first time she laid eyes on Abra. It was during a Hocus Pocus magic act in Chicago where the cat had launched off the stage and into the audience to seek out an obnoxious cell phone. *Clearly the past doesn't repeat itself*, she hoped.

Abra stood up on her hind legs in a meerkat pose. Her head remained motionless, but her ears swiveled back and forth trying to pinpoint where the phone was located. She dropped the ring box at Jake's feet, then ran into the parlor where the judge's purse was lying on the floor. She pounced on it like it was "something good for dinner." Scout joined her and engaged in a tug-of-war; Scout clutched the strap, while Abra clawed the bag.

The judge, not being a cat person, didn't know what to do. She looked at Katherine for a hint. Katherine mouthed the words, "Wait just a second." The judge nodded.

Elsa launched into cat-wrangling mode and made a mad dash for the Siamese. She grabbed Abra, then reached for Scout, but the errant Siamese bit her, and then trotted over to Katherine. Lilac and Abby were positioned on the parlor window valance, craning their necks to get a better view of the Scout and Abra fiasco. "Me-yowl," Lilac cried gleefully. "Chirp," Abby cried softly.

Katherine snatched Scout. "Sweet girl," she said affectionately. She kissed the Siamese on the head, and held her close while Jake removed the ring from her collar. Jake took the ring and handed it to the judge. He then picked up the jeweler's box, and handed that to her, as well.

Katherine motioned Tommy to take Scout to the carrier in the next room. Tommy, in his rented tuxedo, looked very dapper, and older than his twelve years of age. He took Scout from Katherine's arms, draped Scout unceremoniously over one shoulder, and disappeared around the corner. Scout protested the entire way. Tommy spoke very quietly to calm her down. "You're such a cutie," he said.

Elsa was busy. Struggling to maneuver in her high-heeled sandals — worn only to impress the wedding photographer — she'd already jogged with Abra into the next room, and put her in the carrier. Now she had to find Miss Siam.

First, she looked behind the Eastlake hall tree. No Iris. Then, she caught the flick of a pencil-thin tail nearby, thumping on the floor. Iris was hunkered underneath Cokey's chair, and with her delicate brown paw, was extracting his wallet out of his back pocket. Cokey didn't have a clue what was going on, but sat whispering to Margie about how hungry he was, and that he couldn't wait for the reception.

Elsa swooped down, snatched Iris, and held the Siamese in her arms. Iris protested with loud caterwauling the entire way upstairs to the playroom. Elsa thought she needed double pay for her services, but giggled at how clever Katz's cats were. She wasn't out of deep water yet; somehow she had to get the other two down from the valance. She lamented, *That's just what Katz needs right now, for me to put up a ladder.*

The judge cleared her throat, then said to Jake and Katherine, "These rings mark the beginning of a journey filled with wonder, surprises, tears, laughter, grief, and joy.

May these rings glow with the warmth and life that flows through their wearers today." She placed Jake's ring in Katz's hand.

Katherine turned to Jake and lovingly looked into his brown eyes. "With this ring, I give you my heart. From this day forward, you shall not walk alone. May my heart be your shelter, may my arms be your home."

The judge handed Jake Katherine's ring.

Jake said, "Katz, I give you this ring as a symbol of my trust, my faith, and my love for you."

The judge said joyfully, "By the power vested in me by the State of Indiana, I now pronounce you husband and wife. You may now kiss the bride."

Jake didn't need any prompting. He swept Katherine into a kiss that went on for more than the customary few seconds. Daryl pulled Colleen into an embrace and did the same. The wedding guests stood up and gathered around the happy couples. Grandpa

Cokenberger was the first to congratulate the pair, followed by Cora and Johnny. Mum planted a kiss on Katherine's cheek and said, "T'was perfect. May you always be happy."

Chapter Eight

Russell Krow snapped several more photos of the bride and groom, then followed the judge with his eyes. She was leaving. She'd already cleared the door to the back office, and was about to take the stairs to the basement. Obviously, she had parked in the rear of the mansion.

Russell wanted to talk to her. He wanted to set things right. He knew he should take more photos of the wedding party, before they left for the reception, but his need to talk to Janet was far greater. What would Katz and Jake do anyway — fire him? It was a little too late to do that. Besides, he thought, he'd make up for the lost photos at the reception, where he'd be taking pics by the hundreds.

"Janet, wait just a second," he said to the judge. He rushed over to her side.

The judge glared at him. "I want nothing to do with you." She headed down the stairs.

Russell followed her. "Wait! Dammit, woman, would you *just* give me a second?"

"Why, so you can tell me more lies?"

"What are you talking about?" He caught up with the judge and seized her by the arm. "Come with me." He pulled her deeper into the basement.

"What are you doing? Let go of me," she said, struggling.

"Let's have a little fun before we go to the reception," he said seductively.

"Listen, I know you've been cheating on me. Everyone in town is talking about what a fool I am for dating a younger man. But they neglected to tell me you've been seeing other women, particularly that gal upstairs who takes care of Katz's cats."

"You're nuts," Russell said, almost affectionately. "Who told you this pack of lies?"

"Shhh," the judge whispered. "I hear someone coming."

Chapter Nine

Katherine pinched the side of her dress and hiked it up a few inches above her knee, so she wouldn't trip and take a nose dive down the steep basement steps. "Judge, are you down there?" she called. At the foot of the stairs, she turned right, and noticed the half-bathroom door was closed. She could see light underneath the door and assumed the judge was in there.

She knocked, but there wasn't an answer. She knocked again, "Judge, I have your bag."

When she didn't hear an answer, she tried the doorknob, but it was locked. "Who's in there?" she asked. She knocked on the door again, then jiggled the knob.

"Whatever," she said, in exasperation, turning away. She thought she heard people whispering farther in the basement.

"Who's back there?" Katherine demanded. Starting to walk back, she stopped when she smelled a strong odor behind her. She couldn't readily identify it. Was it perfume? Perhaps, the judge's perfume? *No, it couldn't be her perfume*, she thought.

The odor had a pungent, sweet smell, and was almost medicinal. She followed the scent to the classroom and was alarmed to see the exterior door standing wide-open.

Scout and Abra stood on the threshold. When they saw her, they began swaying back and forth, in a macabre dance. Scout's pupils were mere slits, and Abra's eyes were glowing red.

"Waugh," Scout shrieked. Abra growled a deep-throated growl.

Katherine had seen the death dance before. It always terrified her.

She slowly walked toward them, speaking in a soothing voice. "Come to me, my treasures."

Scout arched her back like a deranged Halloween cat and began hopping up-and-down. Abra mimicked Scout's movements.

Katherine inched her way to the upset Siamese. "Come here," she said with a comforting tone. She knew from experience that if she made a false move, they'd do the opposite of what she wanted, and run outside.

The Siamese turned on their back legs, and darted out of the house.

Katherine hurried out, frantically calling for them. "Scout, Abra. Come here." She hadn't seen in what direction the cats had run.

She scanned the back parking lot for the Siamese. Three vehicles were parked there: a shiny black Dodge Ram pickup, Jacky's rental car, and the judge's Corvette. She wondered why Stevie was at Mrs. Harper's next door when he'd told her the job was done. Why was Jacky's rental car there? Where was he? He certainly wasn't at the wedding.

She worried the cats could be hiding underneath any one of the vehicles. She approached the judge's car first. *This is odd,* she thought. *Where's the judge? She's not in the house. Where is she?* She put her hand on the driver's side door handle and started to open the door.

From the corner of her eye, she saw movement. She turned and saw a translucent shape gliding toward the carriage house. In a matter of seconds, it changed into the figure of a teenaged girl. It was the same apparition she'd seen at the yellow brick Foursquare. Katherine wondered why it would be haunting her back yard. The spirit urgently beckoned Katherine to follow. Her feet were not touching the ground, but her hand was pointing toward the carriage house. *No,* Katherine thought. *She can't be real. Why is she pointing at the carriage house?*

Katherine's eyes widened in terror and disbelief. She couldn't believe what she was seeing. At first, she thought she was imagining things, until she realized the Siamese were stalking the specter.

Scout and Abra were crouched down, their heads hung low, shadowing the ghost, and poised to pounce at any second. Their tails were bushed out, and fur stood up on their backs. When they saw Katherine, they dashed right through the ghost, and into the carriage house. The girl's ghost disappeared in front of Katherine's eyes.

Katherine began trembling; she was too shocked to hear someone step up behind her. A strong, muscular arm seized her around the neck and pulled her back. With the other hand, he positioned a rag over her mouth and nose. It was the sickening sweet scent she'd smelled earlier. She struggled for a moment, then lost consciousness.

The man looked around to see if anyone had observed him, and when he was satisfied the coast was clear, he carried Katherine to his pickup truck. He laid her down on the truck bed.

He eased calmly and smoothly into the driver's seat, as if he'd done this act of kidnapping a million times before, and fired up the engine. He was too busy checking out the parking lot to notice a svelte, brown-masked cat with a slender whippy tail sprint from the carriage house. The Siamese leaped effortlessly into the back of the truck, and burrowed underneath a painter's tarp.

The kidnapper put the truck in gear, and drove to the service alley behind the mansion. He had to get the judge to the abandoned storm cellar before the chloroform wore off. He was completely oblivious to the bridal dress worn by the unconscious judge, but he wasn't paid to notice those things. His job was to take "the package" from Point A to Point B. If he screwed up, he'd have hell to pay. The boss lady didn't like mistakes.

Chapter Ten

Jacky, dressed in his black suit, staggered out of the mansion's basement bathroom, and stumbled against a garbage cart. The bin fell and lay on its side with its contents strewn across the floor.

He was so intoxicated, his hands shook when he reached in his pocket for a pack of Marlboros. Opening the box, he plucked one out with his teeth, and struggled to strike a match to light it. Having mastered that task, he lit his cigarette, then flicked the still-burning match. It landed very close to a pile of oily rags. Taking a long drag, he inhaled deeply, then blew the smoke out, through his nose. He thought he heard someone talking, farther back in the basement.

"Katz? Are you back there?" he slurred.

Russell Krow suddenly appeared in the doorway. His hair was tousled, and his black suit had a patch of dust on the front lapel. He didn't notice Jacky at first. He was too busy brushing the dust off his jacket. With the other hand, he held a laptop computer.

"Who are you?" Jacky demanded.

"You startled me," Russell said nervously, rubbing his hand through his hair. "I hate to tell you this, but the wedding is over. Everyone's headin' to the reception. Need a lift?"

"That doesn't tell me what you're doin' down here, does it?" Jacky asked belligerently.

"Listen, I'm in a hurry. I've got to get to the armory to take more pictures."

Jacky was sober enough to know something was off with this guy. "So why are you still here?"

"I left my laptop down here."

"Why would you leave it in a dusty, old basement?" Jacky persisted.

"I best be off," Russell said, heading for the classroom door. "See ya."

Jacky started to follow him, but teetered, and almost fell. The room was whirling around him. He grasped the stair handrail for balance. He thought, *What an eejit, I am. I was headin' to the weddin', but that bloke at the pub kept buyin' me pints. What did he say his name was? Sammie? Sam? I think the arse was deliberately delayin' me so I wouldn't come.*

Sitting down, he smoked more of his cigarette, lurched forward and passed out. The cigarette fell from his hand and rolled toward the rags, providing double whammy to a very unsafe situation — flammable material next to the gas water heater.

When the explosion happened, Jacky didn't know what hit him. The shock wave flung him through an open door and into a smaller room. The thick, limestone inner wall protected him from the fire and serious injury.

The loud noise woke him out of his stupor. At first he thought he was just fine, but when he tried to get up, Jacky realized he couldn't walk. The pain in his leg was debilitating. "Shite," he cursed. From the next room, he thought he heard a woman cry out in pain. "Help me," she cried, then was quiet.

"Katz," Jacky yelled. "Stay where you are. I'll come and get you."

Chapter Eleven

The mechanical room was full of bricks, boards, and jagged shrapnel from the exploded water heater and other debris. The door to the classroom was blocked by an overhead structural beam. Fire danced into the room, and reared its ugly head to the office and sunporch above.

Upstairs, the only people remaining in the house were Jake and Elsa. Everyone else had left for the reception.

When the blast occurred, Jake was in the atrium. Recovering from the shock of the blast, he shouted upstairs to Elsa. "Are you okay?"

Elsa appeared on the top step. "Yes, I'm fine," she said, in a voice bordering on hysteria. "What happened?"

Ignoring Elsa's question, Jake asked desperately. "Is Katz up there?"

"No, when you went outside with your grandparents, Katz said for me to tell you she'd gone to the basement — "

Jake abruptly cut her off. "Elsa, put the cats in their carriers, and get out of the house. I'll get Scout's and Abra's and meet you out front."

Dashing into the living room, he slid on the front metal gate of the cat carrier. Somehow it had detached from the carrier itself. When he peered inside, he was horrified to find it empty.

He raced to the back office to the basement door, and felt the doorknob. It was extremely hot, so he didn't open it. He knew if he did, the flames would rush into the room. He extracted his cell phone and tapped 911. Later, he told Chief London that he was on autopilot, and didn't even remember calling the fire in.

Sprinting back to the atrium, he found Elsa struggling down the stairs with two cat carriers. Inside, the cats were hysterical; Lilac was me-yowling loudly, Iris was shrieking. Poor Abby was alone in the second cage, so traumatized, she was lying on her side, breathing rapidly. Jake grabbed the handles of both carriers. "Elsa, get the door."

Elsa bounded to the front door and opened it. Jake ran outside and nearly jumped off the front porch, taking two steps at a time. He carried the crates next door to the front porch of the Foursquare, and set them down. He hurriedly turned the key in the lock and opened the door, then said, "Stay with them until I come back."

"Wait! What about Scout and Abra?"

"Their carrier was *empty*," he spat, giving her an angry look.

Elsa's jaw dropped, and realized Jake was accusing her of not securing the gate, then yelled, "Jake, you can't go back in there."

Jake didn't stick around to disagree. He cut across the yard between the two properties, and ran at breakneck speed to the basement back door.

The explosion had broken the classroom windows, and angry flames whipped through the openings. Jake saw it was futile to try to get inside through the classroom as long as it was burning.

Close to the door was a fire extinguisher; he seized it and pulled the pin. Stevie ran over from Mrs. Harper's with an extinguisher in his hand. The two men put out the fire in the classroom, but couldn't move any further. The inner door to the basement was blocked by a heavy support beam.

"Is there anyone in the house?" Stevie shouted.

Jake fell to his knees. "Please, dear God, don't take Katz away from me."

Chapter Twelve

Chief London and his wife, Connie, arrived at the reception early, and were sitting at one of the round tables closest to the armory's door. The table was elegantly appointed with a crisp, white table cloth. The centerpiece was a bottle of pink champagne, sitting on a gleaming silver tray with six crystal flutes. Next to the champagne was a bottle of non-alcoholic sparkling wine for non-drinkers, as well as carafes of sweet tea and lemonade.

Mark Dunn and Linda Martin were sitting there as well; they held hands. The two couples were engaged in "catch-up talk," especially with Mark, who no longer lived in Erie, but wanted to hear the latest news, AKA gossip.

Other guests mingled by the front door. Mum and her date, James O'Ferrell, were talking to Cokey and Margie.

Shelly and Tommy ventured to the center of the room, circling the table where the wedding cake sat, in awe of the cake's three layers of creamy white icing. Edible

silver beads cascaded down the sides. On the top tier was a

ceramic bride-and-groom. Tommy reached into his tuxedo

pocket and drew out a miniature-porcelain Siamese cat. He

wiped it off, and placed it in front of the couple. Shelly

launched into a fit of giggles.

Grandpa and Grandma Cokenberger had just

arrived, and were seated at a long table with their family.

Jake's dad was sitting next to Grandpa, but Cora refused to

sit down. She was nervously fidgeting, giving last-minute

instructions to the wait staff. Daryl's parents sat down

across from each other, next to Cora's seat.

When the blast occurred, Daryl and Colleen had just

stepped inside the door.

"Oh, the Saints preserve us. What was that?"

Colleen asked nervously."

Daryl answered, "Something just blew up, and it

sounded very close."

Chief London lunged off his chair, rushing to answer a call on his cell, while the Erie fire department's siren began to wail. Stevie Sanders ran in, and spoke to Daryl and Colleen first. "There's been an explosion at the pink mansion. Where's Katz?"

Cora overheard Stevie, and rushed over. "Jake and Katz haven't arrived yet. What's going on?" she asked in a shrill, frightened voice.

Daryl put his arm around the distraught woman, "Shhh, Aunt Cora. Let me get to the bottom of this."

"What about Katz?" Colleen asked Stevie.

"Are you sure she ain't here?" he asked worriedly.

"Let's talk outside," Daryl said, taking Stevie by the arm.

Stevie shrugged Daryl's hand off. "Talk about what?" he asked insolently.

Chief London joined them and eyed Stevie suspiciously.

147

Stevie speedily sized up the situation, and knew he'd become a person of interest. "Let's not get your Jockeys in a wad. When Jake and I put out the fire in Ms. Kendall's classroom, and found out we couldn't go any further, Jake asked me to come and see if she's here."

With red lights flashing, Officer Troy arrived in his cruiser. Chief London ran over and climbed in. He called back to Stevie, "Son, I'll want to speak to you later."

Stevie looked at him incredulously, then glanced back at Daryl. "We need to help Jake." After he finished his sentence, Cora ran over. "I'm coming, too." Before anyone could protest, she collapsed on the floor in a dead faint.

Johnny hurried over, and started patting her face. Cora came to and said, "Just go without me. Go! Go now!"

Johnny said to Daryl, "Where's your car?"

"Over there," Daryl pointed.

"I want to go, too," Colleen insisted, tagging along.

Daryl turned to her and said firmly, "Stay here with your mom, and try to calm everyone down. We don't want everyone and their brother rushing to the mansion. I'll call you as soon as I can."

"Oh, you will, will you?" Colleen said angrily. She turned on her heels, and stomped over to Mum and her date. She flipped her hair back in anger, "Really? 'Stay here,' he says," then to James, "Where are you parked? We've got to get to the mansion. We need to find Katz."

Chapter Thirteen

Katherine slowly regained consciousness, and tried to get her bearings. *Where am I?* she wondered. *Why is it so dark? What am I doing here?* She panicked.

The floor was cold and damp, and the room had a moldy smell. She rose on all fours, and began crawling, checking out the perimeter. She surmised the area wasn't more than six-by-six feet. She bumped her head on something metal. "Ouch," she said. Rubbing her forehead, she hoped she hadn't been cut, then noticed her crystal foreband was missing. She hurriedly felt her neck. Her tanzanite necklace was gone, too.

Reaching up, she discovered the metal object was a cot of some kind. She felt the coils of the box springs, but it didn't have a mattress or cover. She struggled to stand up, then sat down on the cot. Her head was swimming, and she suddenly felt very nauseous.

Leaning over the edge of the cot, trying not to be sick, she went over the events of what happened after the ceremony, when she tried to return the judge's bag. She remembered seeing the purse on the floor, and telling Elsa she'd be back in a minute. She'd gone into the living room to check on Scout and Abra, and was horrified to find they'd gotten out of their cat carrier, which was impossible because it was brand new. She'd put it together, and tested the tabs that held the two halves together. Elsa or Tommy must have put the cats in, and not tested to make sure the metal gate was secure.

From where she had been standing at the mansion, she could see the living room door to the back office was open. The feline escapees must have fled the living room, then ran into the office, kitchen, or sun porch. Walking into the office, she had been alarmed to see that a guest had left the office door to the basement open. *Why would anyone do that?* she thought angrily. *It had to have been someone who'd never been to the house — someone*

without pets. Judge Hartman, she surmised.

The bout of nausea subsided, so Katherine sat back on the cot, and tried to figure out why she was in this god-awful place. She remembered walking into the classroom, and being horrified that the exterior door was wide-open. But why were the Siamese lingering on the threshold? They had plenty of time to escape. It was like they were waiting for her. And why the death dance? *Am I going to die* . . . Katherine wondered, stifling a sob, *On my wedding day?*

***

Earlier, the kidnapper had parked his black Dodge Ram in the parking lot behind the pink mansion. His orders were to wait for the judge, who would be driving a red Corvette. When she got out of her car, he was to kidnap her. Simple plan. He'd never done it before, so he rented movies on the subject. It didn't seem too difficult.

However, when he drove up, the woman had already arrived, and was inside the house. No one was in the car.

"Damn!" he said angrily. "I'm late." He hesitated to call the boss, and explain the new development. When he did get the courage to tell her, the boss tore into him like a house on fire. She told him to wait until the judge came out, then grab her. After that little obstacle, he was relieved that nothing else went wrong.

When he arrived at the designated delivery point — an abandoned county insane asylum — he noticed his contact's car parked outside a secondary building, which once was the caretaker's home. He was surprised that she'd gone inside, because the place gave him the willies.

The main building, where Erie County sent their most dangerous, criminally insane patients, was two stories of limestone block. A fire in the 1960s destroyed the interior, but left behind charred stone walls, giving the structure a bombed-out look. Seven teenaged girls had died in that fire. He remembered when it happened.

"I better git goin'," he muttered. "I don't want her to git mad at me for being late." He drove his truck to the back of the asylum and parked. He walked over to the below-ground-level storm cellar and opened the heavy wood doors, one at a time. He wasn't sure if it was a storm cellar, or if it was used by doctors to put patients in for treatment. "Or punishment," he smiled sadistically.

He went back to the pickup and easily lifted the unconscious woman out of the truck bed. He carried her down the storm cellar's stairs, and noticed she was coming around. She began to struggle. He lost his footing on the bottom step, fell off, and slid on something oily. He caught himself, but dropped the woman. She moaned. He wondered if he should go back to the truck and get more chloroform, but decided to get out of there instead. In the excitement, he'd forgotten his ski mask, and didn't want her to see him. If the plan went south, the last thing he wanted was to be identified. Kidnapping wasn't his specialty; arson was. But the boss lady wanted to keep the judge for a few weeks and make some money. He was terrible at finances. Let the boss figure out the ransom.

Rushing up the steps and outside, he yanked the handle of each cellar door and pushed them closed. He reached for a metal-rod and inserted it into the ancient latch. For added security, he was supposed to lock a second latch with a padlock, but it had gone missing. "Damn," he cursed, fumbling on the ground. "Where the hell is it?"

He didn't see the Siamese — AKA feline Houdini who could open many locks — crouching behind a decrepit shed nearby. Scout stood on the padlock with both paws. Her eyes were red, and her pupils were mere slits. She meant business.

Irritated, the man walked around the asylum to the caretaker's house, which was a dilapidated, single-story building with a rusted metal roof. The house looked like it would collapse any second. He found his contact waiting in the kitchen, drinking a beer. He counted three crumpled empties on the floor next to her.

"Little early to be drinkin,'" he observed.

"Here, let me get ya a cold one." She reached down and opened the lid of a small cooler. Extracting a cold beer, she slid it across the slatted farmer's table.

"Are you freakin' nuts?" he asked furiously. "I didn't come here to drink beer. We need to take care of that woman in the cellar."

The woman snapped. "Didn't you get my text?"

"What are ya talkin' about?" he shouted.

"The deal's off."

"What?"

"He called me fifteen minutes ago. He said it was too risky, too many people around."

"Where?"

The woman chugged the rest of her beer, squeezed the can, and threw it in the corner. "At the pink mansion, you fool! Are we on the same page here?"

"I didn't see any people. I was just there. The judge was gittin' in her car, and I nabbed her."

The contact's facial expression changed into a twisted, angry look. "What woman?" she shrieked.

"The judge. She's in the storm cellar like we planned. If you don't believe me, here's her purse." He threw the judge's bag across the table. It came to a skidding stop in front of the shocked woman.

She opened the bag, and removed an expensive leather wallet. She extracted the Indiana driver's license and read aloud, "Janet Hartman of 45 Oak Street, Erie, Indiana. Brown hair, blue eyes, one hundred sixty pounds, five-foot-three inches. This is her bag, you idiot, but that woman in the cellar is NOT the judge."

"How in the hell do you know it's not her?"

"Because he texted me and said he was with her."

There was an awkward silence, and then the man spoke hesitantly, "That gal in the cellar doesn't match that description."

"Of course she doesn't, you idiot, because she's not the judge."

The man rubbed his forehead, and said, "She's skinny as a rail."

The contact covered her mouth to smother a long chain of curse words.

The man sat down. "Calm down, woman. No need to git your drawers in a bunch. There's gotta be a way for us to git outta this."

The woman abruptly rose from her chair. "'We?' You gotta frog in your pocket? I'm getting out of here."

The man jumped out of his chair with such force that the chair sailed backward several feet, joining the empty beer cans in the corner. He gripped the woman by her arm. "You ain't goin' nowhere. Now *sit* down!"

Fearing for her life, she acquiesced, but sat in a different chair. "Did the woman see you?" she finally asked.

"No. She was knocked out cold. I came up from behind. She didn't see a thing," he explained, then changed the subject. He pulled out of his pocket the Swarovski-crystal foreband and necklace. "I brought you a present — a little peace offering." He placed the jewelry in front of her.

The woman picked up the foreband, and examined it. When she recognized it was a bridal headpiece, she struggled to catch her breath. Finally, she blurted, "The woman who owns the pink mansion was getting married today. I think you kidnapped Katherine Kendall."

"Who? I ain't never heard of her."

"She's a millionaire."

"Well, let's hold her for ransom, instead," he said, still attempting to get out of his earlier predicament with this angry woman.

"Katherine Kendall has a lot of law enforcement friends. You don't want to mess with her."

"All that because she's got money?" he asked dully.

"She's like best buds with Chief London. Now, getting back to the problem in the cellar, this is how I see it. Get rid of her," the woman said with a callous laugh.

"I can't just take her back."

"Figure it out, but keep me out of it. Do you understand?" she asked forcefully. She reached into her bag and pulled out a book of matches. "Here," she said. "Knock yourself out."

Chapter Fourteen

Outside the mansion's classroom, Jake sat on the picnic table beside his dad, Johnny. He held his head in his hands. "This can't be happening," he said, in shock.

The Erie Fire Department had arrived, along with an ambulance; they filled the back parking lot, already choked with vehicles.

Inside the basement, Jacky lay on the floor, screaming for help. A firefighter heard him, and raced to the above-ground, narrow window. When he saw the injured man, he told Jacky to cover his eyes, while he kicked in the thin pane of glass. "How badly are you hurt?" he asked.

"I can't walk," Jacky said, sobering up. "I think I broke me leg. Shite, I know I broke me leg."

A petite firefighter named Sally walked up. "I can climb through the window. Let me assess his injuries, and stabilize him, before we move him."

She kicked in the remaining shards of glass and leaned in. Judging that the distance from the windowsill and basement floor below was a good four feet, she carefully climbed in and dropped to the floor.

"What's your name?" she asked.

"Jacky Murphy. And what's yours?" he asked, storing in his memory that he'd ask her out for a "thank you" drink before he flew back to New York.

Outside the mansion, several firefighters went to the carport, porte cochère side, and with great difficulty tried to break down the heavy oak door. Another group had gone through the unlocked front door, heard the commotion from the dining room, and speedily opened the oak door for the other firefighters. The fire chief, Sidney Black, had assigned them to search the mansion for more fires, and watch for possible hot spots.

Inside the basement classroom, it took four firefighters to clear the jammed doorway. They made their way through the former mechanical room, and then into the dark, deeper part, putting out small fires as they went. The third firefighter in a group of four men was also an EMT. He nearly tripped over what he thought was a rolled-up carpet on the floor, then to his horror, realized that inside it was a woman, severely burned. He spoke into his radio. "We got a woman down. Possibly dead." He set his EMT bag on the floor.

As more EMTs went in through the classroom, Jake couldn't stand the suspense any longer. He lunged off the picnic table, and ran into the mansion. "Did you find her?" he asked the closest firefighter. Johnny, now joined by Daryl and Cokey, rushed in after him.

The firefighter said, "Sir, you can't come in here." He looked at Jake's dad, shook his head, and asked, "Hey, guys, can you take Jake back outside?"

"Why?" Jake demanded, trying to barge through the cleared passageway.

Daryl and Cokey seized his arms, and pulled him back. Jake's dad put his hand on his shoulder.

Another EMT came in, carrying a large orange bag over his shoulder. He knew Jake, and spoke compassionately, "I have to go inside. You need to step aside, please."

Jake's face was clouded with worry. He thought, *Have they found Katz? Is she dead? Is that why they won't let me go back and see her?*

"Jake," his dad said, squeezing his son's shoulder. "Let them do their job. Okay, son? Let's go back outside."

Chief London arrived, and stepped down into the classroom. He heard the EMT tell Jake to step aside. He'd already heard on his police radio that a woman was found, and was most likely dead.

"Jake, I'm sorry," the chief said. "This is a terrible shock to you, but I need you to leave, so we can do our jobs."

Jake hung his head low, and left reluctantly. As he stepped out of the classroom, he headed back to the picnic table, then stopped. He thought he heard a baby crying. Was it a baby, or a cat? The sound seemed to be coming from the carriage house.

"Did you hear that?" he asked his dad.

"Hear what?" Johnny asked, looking around.

Again, a cry sounded from the carriage house — a loud cry. "Raw!" it shrieked.

"It's Abra," Jake said, breaking into a run. He'd barely cleared the door, when he found Abra collapsed on the concrete floor. She tried to get up, but fell back down. Next to her was a dirty rag.

Jake kneeled down, and began examining Abra for wounds. She appeared to be okay, but seemed to be exhausted. He carefully picked her up and held her. "It's okay, baby girl. I'll get you out of here," he said.

"Raw," Abra cried weakly. Her lean brown paw pointed toward an object on the floor.

Still kneeling and holding Abra, Jake saw what the Siamese was pointing at, reached over and picked up a USB flash drive. He dropped it into an inside pocket of his tuxedo jacket.

Daryl walked in. "Is everything alright?"

"I don't know. I've got to get her to the vet. I just found her collapsed on the floor. Daryl, she was lying next to that rag on the floor. Check it out, would ya?"

Daryl stooped down, and pinched the rag on its edge. He carefully brought it to his nose to sniff. It had a pungent, acrid odor. Daryl, having been an ace in high school chemistry and a trained deputy, knew what it was. "It's chloroform."

Abra snuggled on Jake's chest, and purred lightly. Jake said, "What's it doing here?"

Abra lifted her paw and pointed toward the driveway. "Raw," she cried.

Daryl gave a curious look. "Did that cat just try and tell us something?"

Cokey came in, and saw Abra. "What in the Sam Hill? How'd she get out here?"

"Cokey, I need a favor. Can you take her to the vet? We think she's been exposed to chloroform."

"Chloroform? How did that get out here? Oh, never mind. I'll take her," Cokey said, taking off his suit jacket. "Here, let's wrap her up in this like a little burrito."

"I'll do it." Jake took Cokey's jacket, put Abra in it, and swaddled her. Abra looked at Jake adoringly. She blinked an eye kiss.

Jake caught the blink, and said to the Siamese, "You'll be okay. Love you, baby girl."

He handed her to Cokey, and asked, "Where are you parked?"

"In the alley."

"Thanks, Uncle. I'll call Dr. Sonny, and let him know you're coming," Jake said, as he called the vet on his cell phone.

***

When James O'Ferrell left the armory with Mum and Colleen in his Lady Moo truck, the two women were frantic. "Hurry! Hurry!" they both yelled at James, who was already speeding.

The driver shouted back. "What do you expect? It's a milk delivery truck, not a pace car at the Indy 500."

"Tell me again why you're drivin' this?" Mum asked James irritably.

"My Mercedes is in the shop," he retorted.

Before he'd completely stopped the truck in front of the pink mansion, Mum and Colleen leaped out the open side door, and ran. Mum hurried down the driveway, while

Colleen rushed up the mansion's front steps and through the front door. Mum stopped and screamed, "Colleen, get back here," and then to the group of firefighters standing at the back of the drive, "Help! My daughter ran into the house."

A firefighter dashed down the drive to see what was wrong. "What part of the house?" he asked.

"The front door. Go get her."

"Ma'am, there are other firefighters in there. She won't get far, but I'll look for her anyway."

He sprinted off to the front of the house.

"Bless your heart," she called after him.

Mum then walked to the back, shouting, "Where's Katz? Where's Jake?"

Jacky, who had been rescued, was lying on a gurney when he heard his mother. He yelled, "Mum, over here."

Mum rushed over. "For the love of Mary, 'tis a nightmare. What happened to you?"

"It is what it is, Mum. I broke me leg."

Mum's date, James, caught up with them. He seemed to be out of his comfort zone, and didn't know what to do.

"James," Jacky acknowledged, "take hold of Mum, I need to tell her somethin'."

James took Mum by the arm, and she jerked it away. "Tell me what?"

"I think Katz is injured — "

Mum shrieked and ran over to the two firefighters standing outside the classroom door. "Don't you just stand there. Do something! My two girls are inside the house. Help them!"

Chapter Fifteen

It started out being a quiet, relaxing day, the chief thought, riding in Officer Troy's cruiser to the pink mansion. He'd gotten up before his wife, Connie, and surprised her in bed, with a tray of pancakes and locally made maple syrup — her favorite. Then he had mowed the grass, played with their six-year-old German Shepherd, Riley, and helped Connie plant two rose bushes in the garden.

Later, when the couple arrived at the armory for Jake's and Katz's wedding reception, they were pleasantly greeted by two ten-year-old twins dressed in tuxedos. The boys — Jake's cousins from Ohio — handed out wedding mementoes: A photograph of the bridal couple, taken in the mansion's parlor, each bound in a gilded frame. The chief chuckled when he realized the picture also included the couples' seven cats.

Entering the main floor, the chief and his wife moved from table-to-table, searching for their names on engraved place cards. "Oh, we're right here," Connie said. "Isn't it cool that Jake and Katz are at the next table?"

After seating Connie at the table, he'd moved over to the bar and ordered two Mai Tais, a cocktail they'd fallen in love with on their trip to Hawaii — a trip paid for by Katz. Returning to the table, he'd found that another couple had been seated. Mark Dunn, Katz's former estate attorney, was sitting next to his girlfriend, Detective Linda Martin. They chatted about old and new times, as they casually waited for Jake and Katz to arrive and "start the wedding reception show."

Then, all hell broke loose. With the sound of the explosion, the chief sprung out of his chair and rushed to the front entrance. Officer Troy had pulled up, and shouted through the opened window, "It's the pink mansion."

Getting into Officer Troy's cruiser, he had barked rhetorically, "Is the damn arsonist setting off bombs now?"

Officer Troy replied, "A bomber in Erie. That's a first."

A worried voice had come over the police radio, and announced the grave news. "Woman down," the dispatcher said. "512 Lincoln Street. Basement."

The chief said, "How could a woman be down, when everyone left for the reception?"

"Or did they," Officer Troy offered.

Katherine Kendall, the chief thought with a heavy heart. The first time he'd met her, it wasn't under happy circumstances. She'd just moved from New York City into her late great-aunt's house. Dear old Orvenia had the whole town up in arms when she left her fortune to a great niece she'd never met. Poor Katz moved to a small town, where she didn't know anyone, and had to contend with people who were angry about not getting money that Orvenia had promised them. Then, within the first week of living in the pink mansion, Katz had found two people murdered in the basement.

At the time, he had predicted that the normal gal from out-of-town would have booked it back home, but not Katz. She was tougher than nails, but unfortunately, a magnet for murder. He admired her courage, and her ability to bounce back when these terrible things happened. Now with the explosion, he shuddered at the thought of what he'd find.

He cared about her. He didn't want to find her dead. She was a kind soul.

Officer Troy couldn't find a parking space, so he parked across the street. The chief muttered to himself, "Katz, you've paved your way to heaven with your kindness to others."

"What was that you said?" Officer Troy asked.

The chief didn't answer, but hurried down the drive. Officer Troy followed. The chief stepped down into the classroom, and approached Jake.

"I'm sorry," the chief said. "This is a terrible shock to you, but I need you to leave, so we can do our jobs."

He walked past the firefighter into the mechanical room, and then into another. There, lying on the floor, was a badly burned woman. Burns covered her entire body except for her face, which was still recognizable, but turned to one side. A small foreign object was stuck in the back of her neck. An EMT got up and shook his head. "She's dead."

The chief knew the EMT. "Hey, Charlie, is it Katherine Kendall?" he asked solemnly, not really wanting to hear the answer.

"Nope."

The chief was relieved, then felt a pang of guilt for the victim on the floor. "Who is she?"

Charlie answered, "Take a good look at her face, Chief. It's Judge Hartman."

"I'll get a call out to the coroner," then he asked, "Cause of death — acute burns caused by explosion?"

Charlie paused uncomfortably. "Chief, I'm not a forensics expert, but I've watched enough TV to suspect that she died before the fire."

"How's that?" the chief asked, processing the EMT's theory.

"Look around this room. The thing that stands out is there's hardly any debris in here. How would a six-inch-nail end up in her neck?"

"Good observation. Want to work for the police department?"

"Also, we found her wrapped in an old rug. It seems awfully heavy for a woman in her condition to wrap herself in it."

"I see what you're sayin'. Probably someone else was down here, less injured, and tried to help her, by putting out the flames."

"Could be."

"Thanks for your input."

When Officer Troy walked in, the chief took him aside. "We may have another murder investigation on our hands."

"The fire was deliberately set to cover up a murder?"

"Yep."

"Is the victim Katherine Kendall?"

"No, it's Judge Hartman."

"What's she doin' here?" the officer asked, confused.

"Didn't ya get my email? Katz and Jake were married here today. The judge presided over their wedding."

"Okay. Okay. I got it. But why is the judge in the basement?"

"Don't know."

Officer Troy shook his head. "If I lived here, I'd never let anyone down here. It's like wearing a red shirt on *Star Trek*. As soon as ya see it, you know they're gonna get it."

The chief agreed. "Well, this is a fine can of worms," he said. "I'm anxious to hear what the fire inspector has to say."

A firefighter nearby overheard the chief. "Chief London, Inspector Emrich is on his way. He was out in the country investigating a fire at the old county asylum. He'll be here shortly."

"That's a tad bit of overkill. The asylum burned down years ago," the chief noted.

"He said it was a small fire behind the asylum — some kind of storm cellar."

Interesting," the chief said, noncommittally, then to Officer Troy. "Get the coroner over here, and call the State Police. I'm off to talk to Jake."

"Why Jake?" Officer Troy asked, curiously.

The chief looked at him like he'd lost his mind. "Because he thinks that woman in here is his bride. Get it? After that, I'm driving over to the judge's mother's house, and break the sad news. Keep me updated."

"Yes, Sir," Officer Troy acknowledged.

The chief didn't relish notifying next of kin. No police officer wanted that job, but as chief, he usually was the bearer of bad news. It was very stressful and emotional. He could still remember, in minute detail, the first time he had to tell a young mother of three that her husband had been killed in a horrible car accident. What made the current task worse — if that was possible — was that he knew the judge's mom. She was a nice lady in frail health. He'd have to see if one of Erie's pastors would accompany him.

The chief walked out of the classroom, and asked the closest EMT, "Anyone else injured?"

The EMT nodded. "A man named Jacky Murphy."

The chief pulled at his beard. "Is he a relative of Colleen Murphy?"

"Oh, you mean the redhead, Daryl Cokenberger's girlfriend? Yep, he's her brother."

"I wonder why he was in the basement. What's the extent of his injuries?"

"He's lucky he survived. No burns, but a broken leg."

"I need to question him before you take him to the hospital."

"Chief, he's in a lot of pain."

"Give him something. I'll be right back."

The chief walked off and spoke to a group of firefighters putting away their equipment in one of the trucks. "Has the entire house been searched?"

One of the men answered, "Yes, Chief, and there are no other casualties."

"That's good," he said, then in a booming voice, "Can someone find Jake Cokenberger?"

The firefighter nodded toward the carriage house.

"Jake," the chief shouted.

Jake and Daryl walked out. Jake deliberately walked over as slowly as possible. He didn't want to hear the bad news. "Just tell me. Is Katz dead?" he choked on the words.

"No, but Judge Hartman is. Confidentially, it looks like someone murdered her, then covered it up with the explosion."

Jake shook his head in shock. "It doesn't make any sense to me, but whoever did it had to be one of the guests at the wedding."

"Maybe. Maybe not," the chief offered. "But Katz is missing. I'll put out an APB."

Daryl said, "Chief, Jake and I think Katz was abducted. We found a rag with chloroform on it."

"Bag it, Deputy. We need to have the lab check it for prints, and any other useful trace evidence."

Chapter Sixteen

Katherine felt terrible. The pain in her head throbbed; her eyes burned. The moldy odor in the storm cellar was overpowering; the smell alone made her nauseous. Even though the cot she was sitting on smelled equally as bad, she lay down anyway. She thought if she closed her eyes for a few minutes, she'd get up, refreshed, and figure out how to get out of this mess. She didn't count on falling asleep.

Several hours later, she woke up, and felt invigorated. Her headache was gone. The awful cellar smell had mysteriously disappeared. A thin, shaft of sunlight filtered through the slits of the storm cellar doors. Katherine thought the sun was probably setting.

Rising off the cot, she pointed her arms upward, stretched, and took a deep breath. In the corner was a crowbar. *Why didn't I see that earlier?* she thought. She stooped down, grabbed it, and held it to her side as she carefully ascended the planked steps. On the top stair, she peered through the opening, and observed a lock of some sort — a metal rod running through two latches. She inserted the crowbar, and pulled down with all her might. Finally, she heard the sound of something snapping. Flinging the tool to the floor, she pushed up on one of the cellar doors, and flung it open. She ran down the gravel lane. She had to get to a highway to flag someone down.

Occasionally she glanced over her shoulder to see if the kidnapper was following, but when she didn't see anyone ready to snatch her as in a scary movie, she ran even faster. *I can't be having such good luck*, she thought.

She worried. Something was off, and she couldn't quite pinpoint it. Why wasn't someone guarding the storm cellar? Was the person who abducted her lurking nearby, ready to seize her again? Was he or she armed? Would the criminal shoot her, rather than try to catch her?

In a few minutes, Katherine found her way to the front of the property. The weeds were so high that she didn't see the old metal mailbox, nailed to a rotten post, until she almost stumbled into it. Catching herself, she grasped a rusted piece of barbwire, which dug into the palm of her hand. She gingerly pulled her hand off the barb, and blood started flowing down her wedding dress.

Ripping the hem off of her great-aunt's vintage dress, she tied it around the cut to stop the bleeding. Hearing a car approaching, she stepped up onto the paved road. She spotted a shiny, black Dodge Ram, and couldn't make out the driver because of the brilliance of the sun, and the glare it produced.

She thought she saw Stevie Sanders behind the wheel. *I'm safe*, she thought. *Thank God, it's Stevie. He'll take me home.* She felt an uplifting, almost transcendent sense of relief. Soon she'd be at home with Jake and the cats, safe in her new husband's arms.

Chapter Seventeen

Russell Krow, driving his new Lexus sedan, was halfway to the armory when he heard the blast. Simultaneously, his cell pinged a text message, and he pulled off the street to read it. *Explosion. Pink mansion.*

"I can always count on good ole blabbermouth Officer Troy," he said out loud. "Every reporter needs one."

He texted back, *Be there in a sec.*

Perfect! he thought. *That drunk Irish guy must have torched the place. Now they'll never find the judge. Maybe they'll think it's the Katz woman.*

Then he spent a minute thinking about his women. He liked women. That's why he liked to collect lovers. Older unmarried or divorced women were the easiest to get into his bed. They were weak and easy to manipulate.

The judge was so naïve. He could explain away anything, and she'd believe him. But the real estate lady, she was a different story. She had him pegged from the beginning, but she didn't care. *Use me and abuse me*, she'd say. He laughed, then became serious.

Katherine Kendall was a different story, he thought. Once she fell for that Erie hick, she only had eyes for him. He'd tried to get her interested — tried every trick in the book, but all he got was a cold shoulder. With her big money, she'd get tired of Jake Cokenberger and move on. He just wanted to be around when it happened.

Easing his seat back, he lifted his laptop off the passenger seat, and plugged the power adapter cord into the cigarette lighter socket. He began moving the wedding pictures off his camera onto his hard drive. Back at the mansion, he'd already downloaded the "good stuff" onto an USB flash drive, so that he could relive the drama later.

He got his kicks sitting in his recliner, drinking a beer, and watching Erie's finest screw up crime scene after crime scene. In particular, he liked watching that goof fire inspector. The guy was an idiot. Between the inept fire chief and the goof inspector, he couldn't decide which one gave him more comic relief.

While the files were downloading, he reached inside his suit jacket for his USB thumb drive, and was startled when he couldn't find it. "Oh, no!" he said, alarmed.

He hastily began searching other pockets, then got out of the car, and searched his suit's back pockets. No USB flash drive. Nada. He searched the back seat and floorboard, then did the same up front. He unlocked the trunk, and searched in there, too.

"I've got to find it!" he said frantically. His face fell when he realized where he may have left it, next to the judge's body, at the pink mansion. Then, he relaxed, and said out loud, "I'm sure the explosion destroyed it."

Chapter Eighteen

Katherine couldn't see through the tinted pickup windows, so she ran to the passenger side, stepped up on the running board, and pulled the door handle. She was smiling, so happy Stevie was going to save her, until a man grabbed her from behind, and held the smelly rag to her face again.

"No-o-o," she screamed, waking up. She sat up on the cot, sweat pouring off her brow. *I was having the worst nightmare.* Then, she thought she heard a cat wail. It sounded like Scout. *That's impossible. I'm hallucinating.* But something was outside, jiggling the exterior latch.

"Help me," she called in a weak voice. "I can't get out."

"Waugh," the Siamese said.

Katherine got up and slowly climbed the steps, until her head nearly touched the cellar doors. Through a knothole on the left door, a brown paw poked through. She

189

gently took it and kneaded the cat's paw pad. Scout squeezed her finger as if to reassure her that everything would be okay.

She swallowed hard and bit back tears. "This isn't happening. I'm dreaming again. How did you find me?" she asked through the doors.

Scout muttered something in Siamese, pulled out her paw, and went back to jiggling the latch.

Katherine heard the sound of metal scraping, and then a thump on the ground. Scout returned to the knothole, and launched a series of emphatic 'waughs.'

Katherine took her cue, pushed the left-hand door, and opened it. Scout peeked over the other side and squeezed her blue eyes. "Ma-Waugh," she cried, which sounded like "Hurry up!"

Katherine picked up Scout and hugged her. "I love you, sweet girl." She squinted, and adjusted her eyes to the daylight. Glancing at the burned-out shell of a two-story building, she wondered where she was.

Behind her was an overgrown yard with a rusted, barbed wire fence in front. She could make out weathered tombstones; some of them had toppled to the ground. When she looked back at the building, the apparition appeared behind a glassless window.

The teenaged spirit was wearing the same clothes as before: madras blouse with green shorts. First, the ghost pointed to the cemetery, then gestured toward a dirt lane that went around the building.

Scout chattered, "At-at-at-at!" Her tail quivered against Katherine's side.

"You see her, too," Katherine whispered, relieved that she wasn't hallucinating. "It's okay, Scout." She was too frightened to speak any louder. Then the spirit disappeared.

Katherine moved Scout to her other shoulder. "Okay, hang on. I'm going to run faster than I've ever run before." She jogged around the building, in the direction the spirit had pointed. She saw a long, graveled driveway on her left, and a shack on the right, with two vehicles parked in front. One looked like Stevie Sanders' pickup, and the other was some sort of Ford sedan she vaguely remembered. Her gut feeling told her not to seek help there. The people inside were probably the ones who kidnapped her in the first place.

She darted to the lane, but her high-heeled pumps were slowing her down. She kicked them off, and ran on the grassy part of the lane, clutching Scout for dear life.

Close to the highway, she heard a vehicle. She partially hid behind a tree, and watched it approach. It was a shiny, black Dodge Ram. "Oh, no," she said to Scout. "We've got to find another way to get out of here." Then she saw the front license plate — not clear at first, but readable enough to know it was Stevie's logo — Stevie's

Electrical. She hobbled to the edge of the highway, crying

out in pain, as the rocks tore her feet.

Stevie was a hundred feet away, when he saw

Katherine holding her cat. He jammed on the brakes, and

pulled over to the side of the road. "Ms. Kendall, what are

you doing out here?"

Katherine sighed, and said, "Does everyone in town

drive a black Dodge Ram?"

"Get in," he said, ignoring the question. "Half the

county's lookin' for ya."

Katherine stepped up onto the running board, and

opened the passenger side door. She got in, shut the door,

and set Scout on her lap. The Siamese eyed Stevie

suspiciously, growled, then jumped onto the floorboard.

Katherine reached down and petted her on the head. "It's

okay, honey."

"I love it when you call me honey," Stevie said.

"Again, what are ya doin' out here?" he asked, putting the truck in gear, and getting back onto the highway.

"I can ask you the same?"

"I drive around all day looking for good lookin' damsels in distress."

Katherine's internal distrust-gauge began to rise.

Stevie said, "I'm just messin' with ya. I've got a rewiring job a half-a-mile up the road. I'm late, so I'm tryin' to git there. Now it's your turn."

"I was kidnapped in the back parking lot of the mansion."

"Damn, woman. Did you see who done it?"

"No, they grabbed me from behind, and held a smelly rag to my nose, then I passed out. Do you know who owns the property back there?"

"Yeah, the county does. It started out as an old folks home, then turned into a nut house, and ended up being a hush-hush place for unwed mothers."

"What do you mean by a hush-hush place?"

"Years ago, when a girl got pregnant, and couldn't git a husband, her parents would send her to that place back there. She'd have the baby, which would be taken away, then she'd go back home, usually to finish high school."

"That's heart-breaking! What year was this?"

"Don't know. 1960s, maybe."

"Was it one of the buildings torched by the arsonist?" Katherine asked curiously.

"Oh, no, I can tell you exactly what happened. One of the girls was smoking in bed, and set the place on fire. The building was in awful shape to begin with — a deathtrap. It went up like a bonfire."

"What happened to the girls?"

"Well, Ma'am, I remember my mom said a bunch of them died, but their babies were saved."

Katherine became quiet, and started putting clues together. Could the spirit at the yellow Foursquare be one of the girls burned in the fire? Was she an unwed mother who was forced by her parents to live in shame, in a god-forsaken hell hole, then have her baby taken from her? Was she an employee of the Clay family, or her great-aunt Orvenia? Katherine needed to find out, so the young girl could finally be at peace.

"Cat git your tongue?" Stevie asked.

Katherine said wearily, "I've been through a lot today. Being thrown into a storm cellar was the final *coup de grace*."

"What does that mean?"

"Oh, I mean being kidnapped, and thrown in a cellar, was the finishing touch of a very bad afternoon."

"Cellar? In the house?"

196

"It's out back behind the burned building. It reminded me of the one in the movie "Wizard of Oz.""

"Yeah, I git what ya mean. Ya know, if I was gonna kidnap someone I would have found a more secure place. Why ain't you wearin' shoes?"

"I ditched them back there."

Stevie looked in his rear-view mirror, and floored the accelerator.

"Waugh," Scout cried in alarm.

"Stevie, slow down," Katherine said in rising terror. "What's wrong?"

"Somebody's followin' us, and they're drivin' up fast."

***

The woman staggered out of the building, and headed to her car. A flash and small boom let her know that the man had dealt with the kidnapping problem. Then she looked down the lane, and saw a Dodge Ram truck picking up a woman. She started screaming toward the back of the asylum. "Get over here!"

The man ran around the building. "What's the matter with you?"

"Did you check the cellar before you torched it?"

"No, why should I?"

"You idiot, the woman got away. A pickup just stopped for her."

"Damn, we've got to chase them down. I can shoot them, and make them crash."

"Go for it," she said, climbing into her car. "See ya later."

"No, you ain't leavin.'"

"Use your truck. You're not using mine."

He tugged his handgun from the small of his back. Pointing it at her, he said, "You're drivin'." He moved to the passenger side and climbed in. "Hurry up!"

"But I'm drunk," she implored.

"Then maybe that will improve your lousy drivin'."

***

"Oh, no." Katherine started to panic. She reached down and picked up Scout, and held her close. "Turn off my airbag," she demanded. "If we have an accident, I don't want her to get crushed."

"Done," Stevie said. "Hold on."

Stevie tapped on the brakes, slowed down, and veered to the right. He drove between a row of apple trees. The truck hit the side of a ditch, went airborne for a split second, then landed safely in a weeded area. He swerved to avoid a fence post, then zigzagged across a farmer's field of recently harvested corn. Driving through a barbed-wire fence, Stevie found a gravel lane to a farm. Its dilapidated barn stood on the horizon with both of its doors open; Stevie drove the Dodge Ram inside.

"What are you doing?" Katherine asked, terrified.

"We got to git out, and run."

"Where?"

"Over yonder," he pointed. "To the woods, so I can call for help."

Stevie jumped out of the truck, and opened his crossover toolbox. Katherine scrambled out and struggled to hold on to the anxious Siamese. "Scout, you can't get down. Trust me, sweet girl."

"Waugh," Scout disagreed, and continued to wriggle.

Stevie joined them, carrying a nylon cord. He cut a length of cord with his pocket knife, and threw the remaining cord into the back of his truck. He walked over to Scout and inserted the cord into the metal D-ring of the Siamese's collar, and quickly tied it. On the other end of the cord, he tied a small handle. Handing the improvised cat leash to Katherine, he said, "Run to the woods. I'll catch up with ya later."

"How? I don't have any shoes on."

Stevie grunted irritably, opened up the toolbox again, and extracted a pair of flip flops. "Here, it's better than nothin'."

Katherine noticed he'd also extracted a handgun. He stuck it down the waistband of his jeans.

"Stevie, I beg of you. Come with us? There doesn't need to be any bloodshed."

"Ain't happenin. See that bunch of dead trees in the middle of the woods?" he pointed. "There's a path behind them. Follow it to a shack and wait for me."

"No way," Katherine protested. "It's getting dark!"

"Woman, I ain't askin'," he said firmly. "Just go. I'll explain later. Here, take my cell, and pray you get a signal out here."

"Waugh," Scout cried, jumping from Katherine's arms.

"Okay, let's go," Katherine said. Scout took off, running toward the dead trees. Once again, Katherine was amazed at how smart her Siamese was.

"Not so fast. I can't keep up."

Katherine clutched the leash and jogged after Scout, trying not to think about the horrible pain she was suffering from wearing flip flops on the rocky ground. Looking over her shoulder, she could see a dark gray car speeding down the farmer's lane. She wondered where she'd seen that car before. Was Stevie really trying to help them, or was he a part of the kidnapping scheme? There wasn't time to figure it out. Several shots were fired from the car; one hit the Dodge Ram.

Scout scampered at a faster gait, while Katherine struggled to keep up. The Siamese was leading the way, exactly to the area where Stevie told them to go. At the edge of the woods, the cat darted into the cluster of dead trees, then found the path. She stopped abruptly, and Katherine nearly fell over her.

"What's wrong?" she whispered, picking Scout up. Scout swiveled her ears toward the barn. Behind a large rock, Katherine got down on her knees, and held the trembling Siamese. She peeked over, and saw three people in the back of the barn; one of them was Stevie. The other man didn't look familiar, but something about the woman did.

Katherine was startled when three shots rang out in the half-light. She ducked back behind the rock. A volley of other shots sounded, then silence. Not knowing what to do, she slowly peeked over the rock. She was relieved to see Stevie racing toward them, with his handgun pointed toward the ground. When he caught up to them, he said, "Gimme my cell."

Katherine hurriedly handed it to him.

"Did you call for help?" he asked.

"No, I didn't have time."

He punched in the Erie police's number, and said, "This is Stevie Sanders. I need help at Clint Sanders' old farm, off of Highway 41. Send an ambulance. A couple, driving a dark gray Ford Taurus, ran us off the road, and then opened fire. The driver may have been shot; she's lying on the ground. The man with her is armed, and still out there."

Katherine was amazed at how easy it was for Stevie to describe what happened. She could barely get two words out without stuttering in shock, let alone calmly speak descriptive sentences.

Stevie paused while the dispatcher said something. He answered, "Katherine Kendall is with me. She's safe." He started to say something else, but hesitated, then ended the call. "Come on," he said to Katherine, heading down the overgrown path. "We need to hide."

Katherine picked up Scout to carry her, but had only walked two feet when a loud explosion sounded from the barn.

Stevie lunged back, and stood with his mouth open. "The bastard is torching the barn. Oh, hell no. Not my new truck!"

Katherine tried to turn to see who it was Stevie was calling a *bastard*, but Scout dug her claws in her chest. "Ouch," she said in pain.

Scout struggled to get free, so Katherine crouched over her, and held her down, to stop the Siamese from bolting. Looking through the tall weeds, she could see a glimpse of the barn, and the huge cloud of smoke bellowing out of its roof. Inside, a mass of flames consumed the Dodge Ram. Then there was a second explosion.

Stevie grabbed Katherine by the arm and helped her up. "Here, I'll take the cat."

Katherine objected, but was surprised Scout allowed Stevie to hold her without becoming a wild animal — all teeth and claws — like she'd been a few seconds earlier. Instead the cat snuggled against him, and cried a sweet "waugh," which could have been "Thank you," or "Hurry up and get us out of here."

Katherine followed Stevie, hurting from the wounds her darling "treasure" had inflicted on her, but she didn't blame Scout for being frightened. She was, too.

"Watch your step," Stevie warned. "You can't see the deep ruts in the path because of the undergrowth. This path ain't been used in a while."

Katherine tripped on a root, but caught herself.

"And the roots," he snickered.

"Gee, thanks. Where are we going?"

"To my great-Grandpappy's still. Back in the day, he was a moonshiner," Stevie announced proudly.

Katherine thought, *Why am I not surprised? Seems like 'back in the day,' everyone in Erie made booze to make a buck.*

"I'm sorry about your truck," she consoled.

"It's insured," he said fatalistically, "but I'm not so sure about my tools."

Katherine made a mental note to buy Stevie whatever tools he needed. "Ouch," she said, stepping on a rock.

"Want me to carry ya?"

"I'm okay," she lied. Stevie had enough things to worry about. Number one, he was saving them.

They walked into a clearing in the woods where Katherine observed several medium-sized, banded wood barrels, with corroded copper pipes sticking out of them, which snaked into other equally broken-down barrels. A rusted pot-bellied stove was behind them, dangerously close to a shack that had seen better days. The site was littered with broken Mason jars and other bits of debris.

"Watch out for the glass," Stevie warned.

"We can't hide in there," she said. "That shack looks like it's going to fall down any minute." Several young maple trees grew out of a gaping hole in the roof.

"We're not. Keep on walkin.' Believe it or not, we're very close to the Erie town limits. There's a buddy of mine who lives not far from here."

"Can I please use your cell to call Jake?"

"Ma-waugh," Scout agreed.

"Sure," he said, setting Scout down, and extracting the cell from his back pocket. When Katherine leaned forward to take it, a bullet hit the nearby tree, and startled the three of them. Scout darted into the woods.

"Get down," Stevie ordered.

The second bullet shot through the phone, and exited out the palm of Stevie's left hand. The third bullet hit him in the right shoulder, and he crumpled to the ground. Dropping his gun, Stevie moaned to Katherine, "Run!"

Instead, Katherine took the gun, sprang behind the trunk of a huge Tulip tree, and listened for any kind of sound — a leaf crunching, a branch moving, or a twig breaking — that would indicate the shooter's location. She prayed that Stevie was going to be okay, and that Scout had gotten away. She flinched when a volley of shots hit the tree, and then heard the voice of an angry man.

"Come out from behind there. How the hell did you get out of the storm cellar?"

It was exactly what Katherine needed to hear to pinpoint where the shooter was. He was standing only a few feet in front of the tree. She stayed where she was, and held her breath. She waited for the man to step around the tree. When he did, she raised the handgun and shot her kidnapper in the arm. He dropped his gun, and clutched his wound.

"I'll make you pay for this," he said threateningly.

"That ain't no way to talk to a lady," Stevie said. He staggered over to the man, and kicked the gun away.

Katherine rushed to Stevie's side. "You're hurt."

"Help me get my shirt off, so I can use it to stop the bleedin'."

Katherine carefully pulled Stevie's T-shirt over his head. She'd remembered when Jake had been shot in the shoulder, and how he had gone into shock and passed out. *But why is Stevie still standing*, she wondered.

"Thank you, Ms. Kendall, or is it Mrs. Cokenberger now?"

"Yes, it's Mrs. Cokenberger, but you can call me Katz."

Stevie smiled, then became serious, staring angrily at the man lying on the ground.

"Hey, Paul, you made a big mistake settin' fire to my grandpappy's barn. I'll see to it that it's the last barn you're gonna burn in these parts."

Katherine dropped her jaw in startled amazement. Stevie Sanders, whom everyone in town thought was a criminal, saved the day, and had caught the copycat arsonist.

Paul started to get up. Stevie shook his head, "Do *not* git up until I say so."

Katherine asked, "How do you know Paul?"

"Paul's son is being tried for arson," he answered, then said to Paul, "Apples don't fall too far from the tree, old man, do they?"

Katherine chimed in. "I guess you've been the one setting fires around town to take the heat off your son."

"You got that straight," Paul said sarcastically.

211

Stevie offered, "Judge Hartman's presidin' over the case this Monday. And she don't play."

Paul gave a sardonic laugh. "No, she ain't."

"And why's that, Mr. Big Shot?" Stevie asked.

"Because she's dead. Just heard it on the radio. Got herself blown up —"

Katherine moved beside him. "What did you just say?"

"Judge Hartman's dead. She got herself blown up big time."

"Where? When?"

Paul ignored the questions, and said, "I'm bleedin' on my shirt. Do somethin' about it."

In a déjà vu moment of an event already played in Katherine's dream, she tore a swatch of material from the hem of her wedding dress, and started to lean down to help the prone man.

Stevie took her by the arm, and led her a short distance away. "Wait." Then he said to Paul, "This kind lady is goin' help ya. You do anythin' stupid, and I'll shoot ya right between the eyes."

Katherine looked at Stevie's angry face, and suddenly understood why the Sanders' family had a reputation for being formidable. Although Stevie was gentle with her, he was not someone to be trifled with by anyone else.

"Okay," she smiled. "I'll be careful." Katherine moved over to Paul, stooped down, and gently tied the fabric around his arm. He murmured a weak "Thank you."

"Why did you kidnap me?" she asked.

"I thought you were the judge."

"Did the radio say where the judge was when she died?"

"At Orvenia Colfax's old house — the big pink one."

Katherine panicked. "My house blew up?" A wave of terrified emotions ran through her mind. She wanted to run, find help, and get back to the mansion.

"That's what the news said," he answered with difficulty. He clutched his arm even tighter.

They heard multiple sirens screaming in the country night.

"Cavalry's here," Stevie said to Katherine. "I'm sure the chief will press criminal charges against me. I don't know if that woman back there is dead or not; I hope she's not. If she is, I'll be going back to prison for a long, long time."

"No, Stevie, you don't know that. I'll vouch for you. From what I could see, you were defending yourself."

"Katz, the gun I used isn't mine."

Katherine's face dropped. "Oh, no."

A tall, heavy-set man ran down the path, waving a flashlight. "Comin' through," he said in a gruff voice.

Katherine flinched. The man had long, unkempt black hair, and looked like a younger version of Charles Manson. She was surprised when Stevie spoke to him. "Hey, Ted," he greeted.

Ted came over, and beamed the light on Stevie's wounds. "Dude, we gotta get you to the doctor."

"I got some explainin' to do to Chief London, so I better wait," Stevie answered.

Looking perplexed, Ted said, "Are you out of your mind? You can't just stomp out of the woods into the line of fire. Erie cops will shoot you first, and then ask questions."

"How'd you know I was here? I didn't text you."

"I figured so much. Psychic, I guess," he answered mysteriously. Then he spit out a wad of chewed tobacco into the weeds, and laughed, which sounded like a honking goose. "I've got a police scanner app on my cell. Dispatcher said Clint Sanders' old barn was on fire, then something about you and a woman." Ted glanced at Katherine, "That be you, ma'am?"

She nodded.

Stevie said, "That's Ms. Kendall. She lives in the old Colfax house on Lincoln Street."

"You must be the gal who inherited all that money."

Katherine became more nervous than what she already was. She didn't like the last thing Ted said. Was he going to kidnap her, too, and hold her for ransom? Her vivid imagination didn't even want to go there.

Stevie said, "Katz, this is my buddy. He's the one I told you that lives close by."

Ted said loudly. "Yep, I thought I'd cruise on in the back way, and check it out."

"What are you talkin' about?" Stevie asked.

"Erie bad boys need to be forewarned to get out of Dodge. Comprendo? Dude, you're a person of interest."

"I'll go out first," Katherine said, starting to walk down the path. "I'll get help and come back."

"No, you ain't," Stevie protested adamantly. "Word around Erie is that new cop in town, Officer Friendly, is trigger-happy. I don't want you to get shot."

"I'll take that chance," she said stubbornly.

Stevie said to Ted, "Go with her."

"No," Katherine said. "Someone needs to stay with you."

Ted handed Katherine his flashlight. "You the boss. Just don't forgit where we are."

"And me, too," Paul added, in a weak voice.

"Shut up, Paul," Ted and Stevie said in unison.

Katherine proceeded down the path to the area of the dead trees. She called Scout's name, hoping her cat would appear out of the brush, and leap into her arms, but the Siamese didn't appear. *I've got to find her*, Katherine said under her breath, tears blinding her eyes and choking

her voice. *Where is she?*

Chapter Nineteen

Russell Krow, reporter extraordinaire for the *Erie Herald*, was the first official to arrive on the scene at the old Sanders' barn. He looked around at the devastation, and figured his partner-in-crime had set another fire, but this time it was a big one. Not only was the barn burned to the ground, but two vehicles had also been torched.

"Good show, my man," he said out loud, as if he were talking to Paul. "But why did you pick this piece of crap location? You were supposed to burn down the pink mansion, you stupid jerk."

He got out of his car, opened the trunk, and pulled out a tripod. Carrying it, he walked briskly to a safe distance in front of the fiery inferno. He set up a camera atop the tripod, adjusting its height to take in the whole, glorious fire. He turned the camera's shutter speed to a lower setting for night shooting. Checking that the settings on his camera were correct, he began taking photographs in rapid succession.

When the chief arrived, Russell picked up his tripod and positioned it to face the entrance of the gravel lane. He began videotaping the emergency vehicles arriving at the scene. The next vehicle to arrive was Erie's fire truck, loaded to the max with firefighters, many of whom he knew.

Sidney Black, the fire chief, rode up front with the driver, John Landers. Russell questioned whether the driver could even read a map. *Must have good GPS*, he thought cynically. Two ambulances pulled in, as well. Officer Troy hadn't mentioned anyone being injured. He wondered who the buses were for, then noticed the overturned, partially burned Taurus several feet from the barn. He cringed when he saw the Erie Realty sticker on the back windshield.

Russell left his tripod, and stepped over to talk to Chief London, who had gotten out of his cruiser, and was talking on his cell. Russell waited for the chief to end the call before he spoke, "Helluva scene. Do you think it's the copycat arsonist?"

"What are you doing here?" the chief asked suspiciously.

"Chief, when I found out the reception at the armory had been cancelled, I was on my way home," he explained. "When I saw the barn burning, I stopped by to see if anyone needed help. I was the one who made the 911 call."

Two EMTs walked by, and headed toward the Taurus. One of them called out, "Chief, over here."

The chief hurriedly surveyed the situation, and said to the reporter, "Stand back." He stooped down to examine the woman lying on her stomach. "Is she dead?" he asked the first EMT.

The EMT nodded. "She was shot in the back." He turned the woman over, and pointed out the large, crimson stain on the front of her blouse.

Russell spotted a pearl-handled pistol lying in a patch of dandelions. He was reaching down to pick it up, when the chief ordered, "Don't touch that."

"I was just going to call it to your attention," the reporter answered.

Lying next to the pistol was the woman's purse. The chief searched inside for identification, and pulled out her driver's license. "It's Ava Franklin," he said.

Russell tried to lunge forward to the victim, but the chief caught him by the arm.

"Not so fast," he said. "Do you know this woman?"

"She's my friend," Russell said, covering his face with his hands. "No, not Ava," he sobbed.

"What do you want me to do?" the EMT asked.

"Carefully stand back, and try not to disturb any evidence."

Official Troy arrived on the scene, and picked up the gun with a stick. "Chief, it doesn't appear to have been fired. It looks like she was taking the gun out of her purse when she got shot."

The chief made a loud announcement to the growing crowd of emergency personnel and law enforcement agents. "This is a crime scene. Whoever shot this woman may be nearby. Use extreme caution."

"Why would anyone kill Ava?" Russell yelled over the din of emergency crew working the scene.

The chief faced Russell, and put his hand on his shoulder. "I'm sorry for your loss, but this is a crime scene now, and we'll treat it as such."

"I've known Ava for a long time, and I didn't know she owned a gun, or how to use one."

"We'll get to the bottom of this, but for right now, I want you to go home."

"I beg to differ. I'm a reporter. I have a right to be here."

"I'm not asking you to go home, I'm tellin' ya. Don't leave your house. I'll stop by later. We need to have a little talk about the fire at the pink mansion."

The reporter turned on his heel. "I'm going. You just find the bastard who did this."

***

When the bullets stopped flying, Scout trotted back to the scene, but found her human gone. Two men lay on the ground: the one who had helped them, and the other who had tried to kill them. A big, hairy man who looked like a Sasquatch stood nearby. Scout didn't like the looks of him. The Siamese gave the large man a wide berth, and crept back into the weeds. Following the edge of the path to its origin, Scout heard loud sirens, and saw the flashing lights of emergency vehicles. She hid behind a rotted stump, and watched a family of raccoons scamper down the path. They had been frightened by the loud sounds.

After they passed, she trotted to the opening in the trees. Her Siamese eyes were excellent at seeing in the dark. She scanned the area, but didn't see Katherine. She stood up on her hind legs and sniffed, pulling her lips back in the flehmen response. Her sense of smell was even greater than her vision. No Katherine.

Scout became very agitated, and pranced back-and-forth. "Waugh," she cried loudly, her voice echoing deep into the woods. "Waugh," she cried again, and this time she was heard — not by her person, but by a very large crow that flew overhead.

***

Back at the mansion, fifteen minutes earlier, Chief London had taken Jake aside, and said that dispatch had received a call from Stevie Sanders. He explained,

"There's a fire at Stevie's great-grandfather's farm. He said Katherine was with him."

Jake's face went from shock to relief to confusion, "Why would Katz be with him? Is she okay?"

"Yes, but I'm headin' there now. You can come too, if you promise not to get in the way."

"Can I ride with you?"

"No, not in the cruiser. Hey, Deputy Cokenberger," he called, gesturing at Daryl. "Would you please take Jake to Clint Sanders' old place? Stevie Sanders said Katz is there, and she's safe."

At the mention of Stevie Sanders' name, Daryl fired a suspicious look at the chief, then answered, "Yes, Sir, will do." Then, both Daryl and Jake sprinted for the classic Dodge Impala. Daryl fired up the motor, and the two sped to the old Sanders farmstead.

Before the ambulance took Jacky to the City Hospital, the chief questioned him. Jacky confessed to accidentally setting the fire, and the chief believed him. However, that revelation didn't eliminate Jacky as a suspect in the killing of the judge.

The chief wasn't finished with Jacky. He just wanted the man to get medical attention, and to sober up.

After the EMTs left, James drove Mum and Colleen into the city, following the ambulance to the hospital.

Jake was relieved they were gone. He didn't want any drama when the police found Katz. Mum was getting on his nerves with her histrionics. So was Colleen. He knew how close mother and daughter were to his new wife, but didn't want to deal with them right now, or with the drunken brother.

He thought in disgust, *Who flies from New York City to attend a friend's wedding, then ends up getting drunk every day and missing it? It makes no sense. Wait until Katz finds out Jacky set the fire. I'm bankin' that friendship is over.*

Chapter Twenty

When Katherine heard the police and emergency vehicle sirens, she slowed her pace, and tread carefully. The flip flops offered minimal protection against sharp rocks lining the path. Her feet were killing her. She wanted to collapse in the weeds, and just sit it out until the EMTs found her, but thought otherwise when she saw the misty shape of a teenaged girl hovering close by.

The ghost was wildly gesturing for Katherine to keep going.

Katherine nodded, and resumed walking. When she turned, the spirit had vanished into the moonlit night.

Katherine was starting to lose her fear of the ghost. The spirit had warned her several times. She had to find out why.

Katherine found the group of dead trees, and walked out onto the field. She waved Ted's flashlight at the crowd gathered around the barn, and several EMTs saw her. When Katherine saw the men running toward her, she sat down, bowed her head, and cried. Sobbing, with tears streaming down her face, she didn't see Jake coming up fast in front of her.

"Katz," he said softly, joining her on the ground. He took her in his arms, and held her. His heart was beating fast. "Katz, are you hurt?"

Katherine held onto him tight. "Jake," she stuttered. "Scout's missing. She saved me, and now she's gone." Her voice choked, and she couldn't speak.

The couple embraced for a moment, then heard the loud voice of one of the EMTs. "Ma'am, are you injured?"

"No, but follow that path," she said pointing her flashlight in the direction she'd just left. "Stevie Sanders has been shot, as well as Paul Taylor."

Chief London and several officers rushed over with guns drawn. The chief said to the EMTs. "Stand down, until my men clear the area." The officers went into the woods.

The EMTs waited.

The chief asked, "Katz, did Stevie Sanders kidnap you?"

"No, he saved me. Paul Taylor shot Stevie in the hand, and in the shoulder, then I used Stevie's gun, and shot Paul in the arm."

The chief tugged at his beard, "Start from the beginning. And make it quick, and to the point."

Katherine spoke rapidly. "Paul Taylor chloroformed me outside my house, drove me out to the middle of nowhere, and dumped me in a storm cellar. My cat, Scout, got there somehow, and managed to get me out." She paused, waiting for the chief to scoff at that notion, but when he didn't, she continued, "I grabbed my cat and ran to the highway. Stevie was driving by, and I flagged him down."

"That was convenient," the chief muttered.

"He was taking me home when Paul Taylor and some woman drove us off the road."

"Was the woman Ava Franklin?"

"The realtor?" Katherine asked incredulously. "I can't be sure. The woman was behind the wheel, wearing sunglasses. Why do you ask?"

The chief gestured with his head toward what was left of the barn. "I just found Ava Franklin shot in the chest. She's dead, and someone shot her."

Katherine covered her face in horror. She closed her eyes, and thought *Stevie killed her in self defense.*

"Does that mean you saw who killed her?" the chief asked.

Katherine shook her head. "I was hiding behind that big rock over there." She beamed her flashlight in that direction. "I heard gun shots, but it was so dark, I didn't see anything."

The chief's cell rang, and he stopped to take the call. Speaking for just a second, he hung up, and said loudly to the EMTs, "All clear." Then to Katherine, "Okay, I'll get your statement later." He walked into the woods, and disappeared behind the clump of trees.

Jake asked, "Katz, where are your shoes?"

"I couldn't run in them, so I got rid of them. I think I stepped on a piece of glass."

Katherine tossed off the flip flops, and Jake examined her feet. "Your right foot is bleeding. I'll get one of the EMTs to take a look at it." He started to walk away.

"Jake, wait. Stevie got shot saving me. Hold me for a minute. I'm so glad you're here. I love you so much."

"I love you, too, Sweet Pea," he comforted.

"We've got to find Scout, and then go home."

"We'll talk about that later," he said dodging Katherine's comment about returning home.

"Why can't we talk about it now?" Katherine asked suspiciously. "What's going on? That crazy man who kidnapped me, Paul Taylor, said there was an explosion at the pink mansion, and that Judge Hartman was dead. Now tell me true."

Jake took a deep breath. "There was an explosion in your basement — "

Katherine gasped. "Oh, no."

"The fire has been contained."

"I know that Judge Hartman is dead, but was anyone else hurt? Are the cats okay?"

"The fire wiped out the mechanical room, your classroom, and my new office. There's smoke damage everywhere else."

"Jake, the cats? You didn't answer the question."

"Lilac, Abby, and Iris are fine; Elsa took them to the Foursquare."

"Did you say the Foursquare? It's haunted." Katherine was visibly getting very upset. "Is Elsa with them?"

"Yes, she is. You never told me it was haunted —"

Katherine interrupted, "Where's Colleen and Mum? Why didn't they take the cats to the bungalow?"

Jake took another deep breath. "Katz, Jacky came to the wedding late. He was in the explosion. He's okay, but he broke his leg. Mum and Colleen are with him at the hospital in the city. I didn't think to get the keys to the bungalow."

"Wait, go back to the cats. You didn't mention Abra. Is she okay?"

"Abra smelled the chloroform rag. She's at Dr. Sonny's, under observation. He said he thought she'd be just fine, and could come home tomorrow."

"What else are you not telling me? This is a nightmare!" she said, alarmed.

"Judge Hartman's death may be a homicide."

***

A slender black-and-tan dog with cropped ears chased Scout out of the woods, into a field of tall, dying sunflowers. Although the sunflowers were planted close together, Scout was able to dart back-and-forth between the narrow rows, with the dog in hot pursuit. When she reached a clearing, Scout ran to a Shagbark Hickory tree, and easily scaled ten feet. On the way up, her collar tugged, and pulled her backward. The handle of Stevie's makeshift leash had stuck on a jagged piece of bark, which prevented the Siamese from climbing any farther.

"Waugh," she cried in frustration. She tugged again, but her action only made the collar tighter.

Below, the angry dog paced excitedly, looking for an avenue up the tree. He barked in a threatening, low-pitched voice. Scout hissed and bared her teeth. The dog circled the tree, and jumped to climb it, but fell back several times before he abandoned the idea.

In the night sky, a large, black crow circled the scene, and recognized the distress call from the Siamese. The bird *cawed* out an alarm to members of her flock, who swooped in to help. The continuous cawing of the crows was loud, but the dog wasn't afraid of the birds. He continued snarling, and flashing his teeth.

The crows descended on the dog. They swooped and dove, and fluttered their wings. Two of the birds landed on the dog's back, and hung on with their talons. The dog yelped, and flung them off, but his efforts only annoyed the crows, who cried for other birds to join in the mob scene. The dog ran at breakneck speed across the sunflower field with the angry crows chasing him. He wasn't safe until he'd cleared the doggie door, and was inside with his family.

When the dog left, Scout carefully unhitched her claws from the tree's trunk, one paw at a time, and tried to climb down. But the bark she was clinging tore loose, and fell to the ground. She clung on for another second, and attempted to regain her footing, but the tree's bark wouldn't hold her. Scout dropped, and now dangled in the air below the nylon leash, which was still snagged by the bark farther up the trunk. She cried weakly, as the collar remained tight around her neck.

The large crow dove in, and tried to grab the leash with her powerful black beak, but the weight of the cat was too heavy. Scout wasn't afraid of the bird. Instinctively, she knew the crow was helping her. And she remembered the crow from the cabin in the woods two months ago; that crow was the pet of the scarred man.

The crow found the area where the leash was jammed, and feverishly pecked at the site, until the bark shirred off. Scout fell to the ground, landed on her feet, and immediately resumed trying to get the collar off.

The crow swooped down and landed close to the Siamese. Scout lay on her side, and the bird hopped on the leash. With her talons and beak, she worked at loosening the knot that attached the collar to the leash.

When the leash was untied, Scout started wriggling, and pushed the collar with her front paws and one back leg until it finally passed over her head. She licked her paw, ran it over her neck to soothe the pain, then took a deep breath, and cried, "Ma-waugh" in relief.

"Caw! Caw!" the crow squawked. The bird snatched the collar, and rejoined her flock in the sky.

With the threat of the dog gone, Scout backtracked through the sunflower field. She had to return to where the two men were injured, lying on the ground. Once there, she'd pick up the path, and search for her person. Being outside wasn't what she'd thought it was cracked up to be. She wanted to be home with Abra and the other cats.

***

Russell Krow parked in front of the yellow brick Foursquare. Minutes earlier, he had texted Elsa and asked her if she wanted to go for a drink. She declined, and said she was taking care of Katz's cats at the house next door to the mansion.

He checked his look in the mirror, then got out of the car. He double-checked to make sure the doors were locked, because the last thing he wanted was for some Erie hick to steal his brand new vehicle.

Elsa turned on the porch light, and met him at the door. "Hi," she said. "I just heard from Jake. Katz is fine. Isn't that super news?"

"Yes, that's great," he said. "I know you've probably got your hands full cat sitting, but could you do me a favor?"

"Sure, what?" she asked, opening the door, and stepping out onto the porch.

"Do you have the key to the pink house? I lost something of great sentimental value, and I think it dropped out of my pocket when I was taking pics of the wedding."

Elsa shook her head. "The fire chief has declared the house off-limits."

"I know that, precious angel," he said with a voice dripping in honey. "If I wait for the chief to lift the ban, my stuff may be stolen."

Elsa suddenly turned off to Prince Charming, and asked suspiciously. "What is it you lost?"

Russell saw the look, and said, "Okay, I'll come clean. I've lost my USB flash drive. It's got Katz's and Jake's wedding pics on it. If I don't find it, my ass is grass."

Elsa wrinkled her nose. "Oh, that's not so good."

"So, could you do me a big, big favor? Have dinner with me this weekend?" he asked, changing gears.

Elsa knew a con when she saw one. "Actually, Russell, I don't have the key. You'll have to ask Jake for it."

A flicker of anger flashed across Russell's face, then he composed himself. "Okay, no problem. Listen, you better get inside. It's getting cold out here."

Elsa stepped back in, and hurriedly locked the door. She then walked to the back of the house where Iris, Lilac, and Abby were sleeping on towels. She sat down on the floor next to them, and texted Jake. "Russell Krow needs key to mansion. Lost something."

Jake got the text while Katherine was being examined by an EMT. He texted back, "What?"

Elsa answered immediately. "A computer thingy with your wedding pics on it."

"I'll call him tomorrow. Katz and I are coming to the Foursquare as soon as we find Scout. Explain later."

The EMT walked away, and Katherine asked, "Who just texted?"

"Russell Krow wants the key to the mansion so he can go in and look for a USB flash drive."

"He texts during a crisis. Who does that?"

"No, Elsa sent the text. I don't know the details. Katz, Jacky said the last person he saw before the explosion was Russell coming out of the back of the basement."

"That's suspicious. What was he doing there?"

"Don't know, but I overheard Jacky tell the chief he thought that Russell was up to no good."

"Where was the judge's body found? Please don't tell me in the turret room, where Gary was murdered."

"No, in my new office."

"Oh, no, Jake, I'm sorry. Did your books get destroyed?"

"Fortunately, just smoke damage. The fire was put out before it got to them."

Jake patted his suit pocket. He pulled out the USB flash drive Abra had brought him.

"So, *you* have it," Katherine observed.

"Abra must have fetched it out of the basement room, and ran outside with it. She led me to it in the carriage house."

"Led you to it?"

"I mean directed my attention so I'd see it."

Katherine thought for a moment, then said, "That means Russell and the judge were back in the basement together before the explosion. When I went to return her purse, I thought I heard voices back there, but I was too curious about who was locked in the bathroom."

"Who was it?"

"It's a mystery."

Jake said, twirling the USB flash drive in his fingers. "I think there's something on this that Abra wants us to see."

Chapter Twenty-one

After the explosion at the pink mansion, Cokey left his wife, Margie, and their two kids at the armory. Later, Grandpa and Grandma Cokenberger took them home in their 1975 Lincoln Continental. They stayed with Margie and their grandkids until Cokey got home.

When Cokey walked through the door, the family was in the living room. Tommy was lying on the floor, reading a comic book, with their orange cat snuggled against him. Their yellow lab, Oscar, was curled in his dog bed in the corner, snoring. Shelly was cuddled up to Grandma, and looked like she'd been crying.

Margie asked tensely, "Any news?"

"I just got a text from Jake. Daryl took him out to Clint Sanders' old farm. Katz is okay. "

Shelly jumped up, and did a cartwheel, and nearly kicked a lamp off the table when she came down. Margie scolded, "Shelly, don't do those inside."

Oscar woke up, barked once, and then went back to sleep.

Grandma said, patting the sofa, "Shelly, come sit back down."

"Why would Daryl take Jake out there?" Grandpa asked. "Nobody's lived there since the old man died."

"Pop, I don't know, except that Stevie Sanders saved Katz. Somehow they ended up there. Don't know how. Don't know why."

"He's the young feller that came to the armory and asked if she was there."

"Jake asked him to do that, because he hoped Katz was there. A lot of stuff was going on. We can figure it out later."

"That's my cue to leave. Grandma, you ready?"

"Yes, sir," she said, getting up. "I'm drivin', old man."

Grandpa stuck his tongue out at her. "You ain't drivin' my Lincoln."

"Now children," Margie said affectionately to the elderly couple.

Cokey said, "Pop, actually I wondered if you'd stay with the kids for a bit."

Grandma answered, "Well, of course we will."

Grandpa said tiredly, "I'm plum tuckered out. Mind if I lay down."

Margie said, "Sure, there's another sofa, away from the kids, in the family room. Tommy, can you show Grandpa where it is, and get a blanket off the guest bed."

Tommy got up from the floor, and started to walk down the hall. "This way, Gramps."

Grandpa said, "I know where it is. It's not like I haven't been here before."

Margie suppressed a laugh.

Cokey said to Margie, "Do you still have the keys to that house next to the pink mansion."

"You mean the Foursquare? Why, yes, but why do you need them?" she asked inquiringly.

"I'm bankin' Jake and Katz won't be driving to Chicago tonight for their honeymoon."

Margie shook her head. "As soon as Katz finds out about the fire in the mansion, Scout missing, and Abra at the vet, she'll not want to leave Erie, but surely they can't stay in the mansion."

"You're right. There's too much smoke damage. Besides, the mansion is off-limits until the cause of fire has been determined, and whether the judge's death happened before or after the explosion."

"I feel so sorry for Judge Hartman. Poor soul was at the wrong place at the wrong time."

Cokey nodded. "I bet Max Taylor, down at the jail, is doing the jailhouse rock. It'll be awhile before another judge can take over the case where Judge Hartman left off."

"Cokey, you won't need keys. Elsa's at the Foursquare with three of Katz's cats. I just got off the cell talking to her."

"I've got a plan," Cokey announced. "Remember that movie *It's a Wonderful Life?*"

"I love that movie," Margie grinned.

"Let's get some volunteers, and go to the Foursquare and decorate. The hotel is still open; Velma can bring over a prime rib dinner for two."

"Perfect, and I have that fancy Merlot one of my clients gave me."

"Let me make a few calls," he conspired. "They'll need a table and chairs — "

"We've got the card table in the basement," Margie interrupted, equally enthusiastic about Cokey's project.

"Okay, card table, and they'll need a bed."

"I've got that inflatable guest bed. I'll also need to take one of the vacuum cleaners. Let's make a list of what to take."

"I'll call in the troops."

"I'll call in my drywall guys."

"You got it!"

Cokey punched in a number, then said to his wife, "I love you, Margie."

Margie teared up and said, "I love you, too, Cokey."

Chapter Twenty-two

Katherine and Jake sat on the grass, holding hands. Their flashlight was propped up with a broken limb. They watched the emergency helicopter take off from the field close by. Katherine prayed Stevie would be all right. The ambulance carrying Paul Taylor to the hospital in Brook County had already left. A hearse had taken Ava's body to the funeral home seconds earlier.

The chief stood nearby, nervously tugging at his beard. Moments before, he'd finished taking Katherine's statement. Now he complained that no one had found Stevie's gun.

"When I left to get help, the gun was close to Stevie. I assume Ted probably took it, and made sure Paul Taylor didn't try to escape."

"Yeah, that's what you said, but I'm tellin' ya, there was no Ted at the scene, or a gun."

"Stevie said Ted lives farther down the path. We were headed there when Stevie got shot."

The chief shook his head. "Deputy Troy said there is *no* house back there, but a farmer's access road to a metal grain bin."

Katherine wondered why Stevie would lie to her, but didn't say anything.

"We need the gun," the chief said, leaving. "I'll secure this area, come back at daybreak, and bring Officer Shepherd with me."

Katherine knew Officer Shepherd was Erie's police department's German Shepherd. But when the dog was off-duty, he spent most of his time with Chief London and his wife, Connie.

"Chief, did any of your officers report seeing my cat?" Katherine asked.

"No, I'm sorry," the chief said, "but someday you need to tell me how you *really* escaped from that storm cellar."

Katherine gave a wry look, and regretted including Scout in her statement. She didn't want the chief to know how extraordinary Scout was, but now that she had, he hadn't believed her anyway.

Katherine said to Jake, "I cannot leave without Scout."

Jake squeezed her hand. "I understand. Maybe Scout is nearby and afraid of the noise, especially with people tramping about."

"If we stay here, for a while, I'm hoping she'll come out of hiding, and come to me. If not, let's walk the path and call for her."

A large crow swooped out of the air, cawing loudly. She dropped a blue rhinestone studded collar in Katherine's lap. Then, the bird flew away.

253

"I don't believe this," Katherine exclaimed. "It's Scout's collar."

"Okay," Jake said mysteriously. "I feel like this is a plot for a Disney picture."

Katherine got up, and started calling for Scout. "Treat! Treat! Come here."

They heard movement in the grass behind them, then a svelte, brown-masked Siamese trotted toward them.

"Waugh," she cried happily.

Katherine picked her up, and held her close. She buried her face in Scout's soft fur, and started sobbing.

Jake put his arms around them. "My two baby girls," he cooed.

The crow flew overhead, cawed four times, then left.

"Waugh," Scout said loudly, gazing up at the bird.

"We can go home now," Katherine choked.

"You stay here with the flashlight, and Scout. I'll see if one of the officers can give us a lift."

"I can walk," Katherine said, taking a few steps, then limping. "Maybe not."

Chapter Twenty-three

Katherine lay on an inflatable mattress on the oak floor of the Foursquare's living room, with Scout nestled in her arm. Snuggled in the other arm was Abra. Katherine had convinced Dr. Sonny to release Abra the previous night, because Scout was very upset her sister was gone. Both of the seal points were snoring.

Lilac and Abby were huddled nearby in one breathing fur ball. Iris was sitting in a regal pose, staring at Katherine. Katherine woke in a start. Her movement startled the cats, but Iris continued watching. "Yowl," she cried.

"What's wrong, Miss Siam?" Katherine asked drowsily. Iris climbed up and stood on Katherine's stomach.

"I better get up and feed my girls. Where's Jake?"

Katherine carefully rose so as to not disturb the cats, and walked barefoot to the kitchen. Jake was frying bacon and eggs in an iron skillet. "Good morning, sunshine," he said.

She went over and hugged him. "You made me breakfast."

"Yes, Mrs. Cokenberger."

"I love the sound of my new name. I have to admit, I *am* starving."

"You didn't hardly touch your food last night."

"I know. My stomach was in knots. I can't stop thinking about that awful storm cellar."

"Try to forget it," Jake consoled, then said, "We've got to do something special for everyone who brought stuff over so we had a place to sleep last night."

Katherine grinned. "I think Cokey and Margie organized it."

"There's juice in the fridge, if you'd grab it and set it on the table."

The cats padded in. Scout stretched. Abra jumped up on the counter, near the stove, to see what Jake was cooking.

"No, get down," he scolded, then to Katz. "We need to find a room to put the cats in while we're in the kitchen. I don't want them to get burned, leaping up on the stove."

"I think the upstairs front bedroom would work. It can be their cat room away from home. I know they'll miss their playroom."

"Katz, there's a bag over there. Aunt Margie went to the store and bought cat food."

"I love her. She's adorable."

The cats had become very vocal.

"Okay! Follow me," Katherine said to the excited cats. She grabbed the bag. "Oops, what do I use for dishes?"

"There are paper plates and plastic utensils in the bag. Aunt Margie thought of everything."

Katherine led the cats upstairs to the front bedroom, dished out the food, then shut them in the room. Heading back downstairs, she thought she heard a giggle, but hoped it wasn't the apparition trying to communicate again.

After breakfast, Jake and Katherine stood behind the kitchen island and wrote a list of items they'd need from the mansion.

Jake began, "Whatever has smoke on it should be left behind for the professional cleaners."

"I'm afraid to go over there. Can I skip it?"

"Sure, Sweet Pea."

"At least for today. I just want to chill out with my new husband."

Jake gathered Katherine in his arms, and held her. "It's a plan," he whispered in her hair.

Chapter Twenty-four

Jake drove Katherine to the front entrance of the hospital, and braked. "I'll go park, and find you later."

Katherine got out of the Jeep, and headed for the automatic doors. She walked to the front desk, and asked where Stevie Sanders' room was.

"Room 616," the receptionist said. "Just turn the corner for the elevators."

"Thanks," Katherine smiled. She hoped Jake would have a hard time finding parking in the busy lot, so she'd have a few personal minutes with Stevie.

She hopped on the elevator and rode to the sixth floor. Getting off, she easily found the room, which was close to the nurse's station.

She was surprised to see a policeman sitting outside his room.

"Hello," she greeted. "I'd like to see Stevie."

"Are you a relative?"

"No," she said. "I'm a friend."

"You must be a really good friend, because nobody else has come to see him."

Katherine's heart sank. She wondered why his sister, Barbie, hadn't come to see him. She'd texted two days ago and told her he was injured. "Do you need to see my identification?" she asked.

"No, that's not necessary, Ms. Kendall. Chief London texted and said you might be coming."

"Thank you," she said, going in.

Stevie was sitting up in bed. His shoulder-length blond hair was tousled, and he was in need of a shave, but he was still strikingly handsome. His left arm was elevated, with a wrap covering his injured hand. A drainage tube stuck out of his shoulder wound.

"Hey, good lookin'," he greeted her, happily. "You're a sight for sore eyes. How ya been?"

Katherine walked closer, and stood next to the bed, holding onto the bed rail. "I'm so sorry that I'm the reason you're in here."

"I did what I should have done when you were stayin' at the cabin. I guess I paid my debt."

"Not a debt, Stevie. You saved my life."

"And your cat," he said, winking.

"Why is there an officer outside? What's going on?"

"I've got a court hearing in a few days."

"Why? Didn't Chief London notify you that ballistics on Paul's gun showed that he shot Ava Franklin?"

"I was relieved to hear my gun didn't kill her, but I *was* shootin' at her. Got lucky, this time, and missed."

"So, why is there a court hearing?"

"It's a probation deal. I'm sure I'll have to go back to prison."

"Who's your attorney?"

"I don't have one."

"I'll fix that."

"Can't afford it," he said gloomily.

"You don't have to. I'll take care of it."

"I ain't no charity case."

"Yes, you are. You're mine," Katherine said with tears welling in her eyes. "I'm going to take care of this."

"Well, I ain't in the position to argue with a beautiful woman."

Katherine flushed, then said, "Stevie, Jake's on his way up. I wanted to ask you something before he gets here."

"Brought the other half. I like that. What's your question?"

"I need to know," she asked slowly, with caution, "what you did with your gun?"

Stevie laughed, then winced. "Ouch, damn pain, won't go away." He changed the subject, "I'd be outta here already if my shoulder hadn't gotten infected. The doc has me drugged up."

Katherine knew he was avoiding the question. "The chief wants to know who the gun is registered to."

"I told him. It ain't mine."

"Was it stolen? Did you find it? Surely, you know the answer to these questions."

"Yeah, I found it when I reached in my toolbox for the flip flops. Then, I remembered Ted had forgotten to take it back. He helped me carry a heavy furnace into a client's house. He's always packin'. I told him to put it in the toolbox because I didn't want the gun to go off while we were movin' the furnace. The gun belongs to Ted, and it's registered in his name."

Katherine asked impatiently, "But why didn't you tell Chief London that?"

"Judgin' by the way you're gittin' all fired up, I believe it's somethin' I need to do."

"Okay, Stevie, this explains who the gun belongs to, do you think Ted picked it up, and took it home before the police arrived?"

"Ted booked it back home as soon as he heard the sirens."

"And where was that? Chief said there wasn't a house at the end of the path."

Stevie snickered. "I guess I forgot to tell ya. Ted lives in his Winnebago."

"A motorhome? But I remember you telling me we were going to a friend's house."

"Did I? I can't remember. I should have said the motorhome *is* Ted's house."

"Where do you think he's parked now?"

"Parked?" Stevie asked with an amused smile. "I'd reckon he'd be in Alaska by now."

"Why?"

"Ted's on probation, too. I met him in jail."

Katherine thought, *The plot thickens.*

"I'm kiddin'. Ted wouldn't flee the State. Try looking at the Sanders' trailer court. He could be there. Don't know. Besides, it doesn't matter that the chief can't find Ted. I know for a fact he doesn't have the gun, because he left it with me."

"But, where is it?" Katherine implored.

"You won't believe it if I told you."

"Try me."

"Move closer," Stevie said.

Katherine leaned over the bed rail.

Stevie whispered, "A giant crow swooped in and carried off the gun."

Katherine looked at Stevie and furrowed her brow. "That's ridiculous."

"It's true."

"That's impossible. A crow can't carry a gun. It would be too heavy."

"A lightweight handgun could weigh as little as a pound."

"Stevie, please be serious."

"Okay," he agreed. "I swear on a stack of Bibles that what I'm about to say is the whole truth — "

"Okay, I get it," Katherine said impatiently.

"Three of the biggest raccoons I've ever seen in my life came waddling down the trail. Paul screamed at them to get away. Two of them fled into the brush, but one came over and started messin' with the gun —"

"This is even more ridiculous than the other story. Stevie, stop! Why are you *not* taking this seriously? You can be sent back to prison. If the chief has the gun, with your prints and mine on it, chances are you won't."

"Let me finish," he said firmly. "If the chief wants the gun, he can go back to where I was sittin', which was about two feet from a ravine. When I yelled at the damn raccoon, he got startled, started to scramble away, and pushed the gun over the edge. That's the honest-to-God truth. Take it or leave it," he said, his face clouding.

"I'll call the chief and let him know this information. Plus, the little ditty about Ted."

"I'm sorry. I don't want to be mad at ya. Come closer," Stevie enticed, then he kissed Katherine on the ear. "Thanks for comin'. You're a good friend to me."

The police officer stepped in, and called time. "I'm sorry, ma'am, but you'll have to leave."

"Thanks, Officer," then to Stevie, "I'll try and come back tomorrow to see you."

"I'll be here." He winked.

"And expect a visit from an attorney."

"Thanks," Stevie mouthed the word.

Katherine left the room, and looked up and down the hall for Jake. He was standing several feet from the door, leaning up against the wall.

"There you are," she said, smiling.

"I thought you needed some time with Stevie," he said with a glint of curiosity in his eyes.

Katherine hugged him. "Can we go home now?"

Jake kissed her on the forehead. "Yes, Sweet Pea, but we've got to hit a department store and buy a few things for the Foursquare."

Katherine giggled. "Let's see, first thing on the list, sheets that don't feel like sleeping on a burlap bag."

"Yeah, Aunt Margie can have her sheets back."

"We also need to go to the pet store. The cats want cozy beds and not folded towels. They're very particular."

"How about lunch first? I'm starving," Jake suggested.

"Okay, but I need to make some calls while we wait for our food. But while we're heading to the Jeep, I need to text Evan."

"Why?"

"I want to know if a crow can carry a gun."

Jake stopped and looked at her in amused disbelief. "I think I can answer that one — not so much."

"How about a raccoon?"

"Nuts!"

"Raccoons, not squirrels," Katherine joked. She proceeded to tell Jake everything she'd discussed with Stevie.

Jake commented, "There is a hint of truth in what Stevie said. Sometimes the most ridiculous thing is actually true." He hugged Katherine, and helped her climb

up into the Jeep.

Chapter Twenty-five

Katherine and Jake sat cross-legged on the floor of the Foursquare. Jake's laptop was positioned on a cardboard box. Chief London sat on a folding chair close by. Jake inserted the flash drive in his laptop's port.

"I found this on the floor of the carriage house," Jake began. "It belongs to Russell Krow. Russell must have lost it after he'd taken our wedding pictures."

"So how'd it get in the carriage house?"

"I don't know," Jake said, then looked knowingly at Katherine. They both suspected Abra had fetched it from the basement minutes before the explosion. They shuddered to think their Siamese could have been seriously injured.

The chief asked, "Are your wedding pictures on it?"

"No, I don't think Russell had time to download all the pics on his camera onto his laptop. Give my computer a sec to pull up everything on this flash drive; there are a lot of photos and videos on it."

Katherine quietly sat holding Lilac on her lap. The lilac point had become clingy, and was upset by the change in her routine. Abby sat underneath the chief's chair.

"Here we are. Take a look at this last video. It was shot in the mansion's basement. Russell must have set his camera on a tripod or something."

The chief leaned in. Katherine looked away. She didn't want to watch it again. "Oh, what a sick bastard," the chief said disgustedly. "Is there audio?"

"No, can't explain why. Chief, the video shows the last moments of Judge Hartman's life."

The video ended with a short flash and a black screen.

"Is that it?"

"There's more, but this is the only thing on here regarding the judge."

"So, here's how I see it," the chief said, running his fingers on top of his buzz cut. "The judge was fighting him off. He lifted her into an uncompromising position, threw her against the wall, which forced her neck into a six-inch nail. The nail punctured her brain stem. Probably paralyzed and killed her instantly."

Jake asked, "Did he know the nail was there, and do this intentionally?"

"When the EMT found her, she was wrapped in a rug. I think Russell was horrified that he'd killed her, and covered her to prevent others from seeing her that way."

"Sort of like respect for the dead," Katherine added.

"Looks likes involuntary manslaughter or reckless homicide to me. Can I trust you two to not say anything? This is official police business. A warrant has been issued for Russell's arrest, but he hasn't been apprehended yet."

"Contrary to everyone else in Erie, Jake and I do not have loose lips. So your secret is safe with us,"

Katherine laughed uneasily, then continued, "Actually, I feel I have an interest in this because I was involved."

"Fair enough," the chief said, then said loudly, "Gimme that." Iris had appeared out of nowhere and had stolen the chief's cruiser's keys. She dropped them, looked guilty, then fled to the other room. He tipped his head back and laughed. "Stress relief," he apologized. "I didn't mean to show disrespect for poor Judge Hartman, but sometimes it helps clear the air, even if it's temporary."

Jake explained, "Chief, there are several videos of Paul Taylor setting fires, and Russell Krow filming them."

"I should have been suspicious when Russell was always the first one on the scene. Of course, he was, because he was right there when the fires were started!"

"What about Paul Taylor?" Katherine asked. "What's going to happen to him?"

"He's being charged with the murder of Ava Franklin. I was there when he was interrogated. Can you believe he said he shot Ava because of her 'quote' big mouth?" The chief shook his head. "Also, attempted murder, arson, and kidnapping, to name a few."

Jake asked, "What was the realtor's role in this?"

"She was one of Russell's lovers. Several of the properties that burned were her listings —"

Katherine interrupted, "She wanted to be my agent on this house. I'm so glad I said no, or else this place might have been torched. She had access to the keys to those homes that were burned."

"Yep," the chief agreed. "She'd give the key or lockbox code to Paul, and he did his arson thing. Russell was an arsonist by proxy. Quite the threesome, that trio."

Katherine asked, "I'm still not clear on their motives."

The chief answered, "Paul Taylor's son was going to be tried for arson in Judge Hartman's court. He didn't want her as the presiding judge, so with Ava, he concocted the kidnapping of the judge, who would be held against her will, until another judge was found to continue the trial. He said that Russell gave him money to torch the pink mansion, but when he came to the house, he chickened out, and snatched you instead."

Katherine shook her head ruefully. "I could have been in the storm cellar forever."

"Paul said Ava told him to torch it," the chief said. "Katz, I'm happy you escaped."

Jake added, "Paul was setting fires so everyone would think the police had caught the wrong arsonist."

"Yes, exactly."

"So, Chief, this exonerates Stevie Sanders," Katherine said hopefully.

"I wondered when you'd get to that. Yes, Stevie Sanders is no longer a person of interest. We found the gun, thanks to Officer Shepherd."

"Riley?"

"Yes, Officer Riley Shepherd," the chief winked. "It was stuck in a mass of tree roots, in the ravine where Stevie said it was. Riley didn't find it the first time, but the second time we went back, he was all over it like a bad case of poison ivy."

"Are you going to tell Stevie's Probation Board that?"

"You mean, you want to know if I'm going to the hearing. Yep, I'll be there. I think this boy is tryin' to go clean, and I want to help him."

Katherine got up, and went over and hugged the chief. "Thank you. This means a lot to me."

"Well, that about sums things up," he said, slightly embarrassed. "I need that USB." He pulled an evidence bag out of his jacket. Jake took the flash drive out of the laptop and dropped it in the bag. The chief zipped the bag, and returned it to his pocket. "Oh, by the way, I'll try my best to get your wedding photos."

"Thanks. Katz and I appreciate it," Jake said, getting up. "Hope you catch Russell soon."

"I'll text you," the chief said, rising. "I know you haven't had time to look out the window, with me being here and all, but Officer Troy is sittin' out in his cruiser, and will be keeping watch on your house until we do make an arrest."

"That's good to know," Katherine said, following the chief to the door.

The chief turned and said, "Goodbye, cats."

"Me-yowl," Lilac belted.

The chief's cell phone pinged. He moved to read the text. "Speak of the devil," he said. "Well, folks, no need to worry. Russell Krow was just arrested at the Indy airport. He's being transported back to Erie. Alrighty, then," he said, opening the door. "Take care."

Chapter Twenty-six

Katherine drove her Subaru off the highway, onto the long lane of the former county insane asylum. Slowing down to a snail's pace, she powered her window down and leaned out, searching for something on her side of the road.

Jake, riding shotgun, asked, "What are you doing?"

"I'm looking for my shoes."

"Is this where you lost them?"

"I didn't lose them. They were slowing me down, so I took them off. Oh, never mind," she said, speeding up. "The weeds are so tall, I wouldn't be able to see them anyway. Maybe on the way back, we can get out and look."

"Sure, but do you think Stevie's raccoon got them?" Jake asked, tongue-in-cheek, deliberately trying to calm Katherine down.

Katherine made a face. "Oh, possibly, or maybe Evan's crow took them."

"Just messin' with ya."

Katherine drove farther down the lane, around the dilapidated building, and parked behind it.

Scout sat in her carrier on the back seat. "Waugh," she protested for the fiftieth time since they left Erie.

Jake climbed out and opened the door to extract the noisy Siamese from the carrier.

Katherine came around and inserted the leash into Scout's harness. She picked up the cat, and set her on the ground.

"Okay, sweet girl, let's take a walk."

Jake reached into the glove compartment and removed his Glock. He turned and placed it in his back holster.

"I didn't see you put your gun in there," Katherine said, surprised.

"I'm making sure my two girls are safe," he smiled. "Sweet Pea, these days I'm always packin'."

Scout trotted toward the storm cellar, then stopped. A clump of grass caught her feline attention. She pulled several blades, and began to munch on them.

Katherine pointed. "Jake, that's the infamous cellar where that nutcase Paul Taylor took me."

"Looks like the storm cellar in the Wizard of Oz."

"I know. That's what I thought. I think I'll skip giving you the grand tour."

"Well, with the official crime scene tape closing it off, I don't think it's a good idea for anyone to go down there."

"It's hard to believe a county-owned building would have such a small cellar. It's a very small space. It wouldn't accommodate many people."

"It could have served other purposes as well, but I think it would be too ghoulish to imagine for what," Jake noted. "Is that the cemetery?"

Scout cried, "Ma-waugh," and tugged at the leash.

"Take us there, sweet girl."

The couple walked through tall grass until they got to a rusted, barbed wire fence. Scout scooted underneath it, but Katherine stopped. "Wait a minute, Scout."

"Hang on," Jake said, walking over. He grabbed the wire. "I'll hold it up until you clear." After Katherine had crawled to the other side, he easily stepped over it.

Katherine and Scout made their way to the neglected cemetery. Scout began sniffing the air. She stood on her hind legs, and partially opened her jaw.

"According to my research," Jake began, "the State closed the asylum in 1962."

"Is that when it became the home for unwed mothers? Stevie called it the hush-hush place."

"Yes, I'm afraid so. Back in the 1940s, 50s, and early 60s, having a child out-of-wedlock carried a negative social stigma."

"When Scout rescued me from the cellar, we both saw the same apparition that has been haunting the Foursquare. At first, the spirit pointed toward the cemetery. I think she died here, either in the fire, or for some other reason."

"Since we don't know her name, let's concentrate on tombstones from the 1960s."

"I don't understand why anyone would be buried here, and not at the Ethel cemetery?"

"I suspect that many were very poor, and wards of the State."

"That's so sad."

Scout led Katherine around the perimeter of the gravesite, then zeroed in on a row of flat stone markers on the ground. Katherine kneeled down next to one, and pulled away the vines that partially covered it. Scout helped. "1965," she said excitedly. She quickly counted the number of tombstones in the row. "Seven," she said.

"Read off the names, and I'll write them down," Jake said, taking out a small notebook.

"Marsha Goodman, died October 3, 1965."

"I think we're on to something. Isn't that the date of the fire?"

"Yes, according to the newspaper article. The marker doesn't show a birth date, just the year she died."

Jake shrugged. "Keep going."

"Lesley Adams, died October 3, 1965."

"The folks who ran the home must have saved money by not engraving the birthdates."

"Susan Deeds. This is crazy," Katherine said. "Where were these girls' families?"

Scout was interested in the next marker. She rubbed her face on the stone, and then began furiously digging.

"Stop that," Katherine scolded, moving in to pick her up.

Scout straddled a white object.

"What do you have there?" she asked, leaning in.

Scout kicked the object with her back leg. It tumbled a few inches, and landed on the toe of Katherine's sneaker.

"Whoa, Jake, it's one of my wedding shoes! What's it doing here?"

"Where's the other one?" he asked.

"It's on top of the grave marker," Katherine said, surprised. She reached down and lifted up the other shoe.

"That's strange. Whose grave is it?"

"I can't make out the name," she said, then shuddered. She looked up at Jake with a shocked expression on her face. "Katrina Doe. Died October 3, 1965."

"Katrina? Didn't you say that was the name of Evelyn Clay's daughter?"

Katherine nodded. "I've heard of Jane Doe or John Doe."

"Yeah, it's usually the name of a patient or a deceased person whose identity is unknown."

"Could this be Katrina Clay's grave?" Katherine asked, hopefully.

"Ma-waugh," Scout agreed.

Jake leaned down, and removed the vines covering the lower part of the marker. "This gravestone has a birthdate. January 15, 1951."

Katherine gasped, doing the math in her head. "She was only fourteen-years-old."

"Is this Katrina Clay's birthdate?"

"Don't know. I'll have your great-uncle, down at the courthouse, help me." Katherine sat down, and held Scout on her lap. "Jake, my gut instinct tells me this is Katrina's grave. She was fourteen-years-old, unmarried, and pregnant. She wanted to keep her baby."

"How do you know that?"

"Because the first time I saw her, she was clutching a baby blanket," Katherine said, then continued, "Her mother didn't want her daughter shamed by people in town — "

"Or Evelyn Clay didn't want to be shamed," Jake finished.

"She banished her *only* child to this horrific place for unwed mothers, so Katrina could have the baby, and put the child up for adoption. Then, Katrina could go back home, and carry on like nothing ever happened. What kind of parent would do such a thing to her *own* child?"

"I'm sorry to say, it was the cultural norm back then," Jake said, shaking his head. "It's a mystery why Katrina was buried here without the town knowing about it."

"Evelyn Clay told everyone her daughter was attending a finishing school in Massachusetts. There was even an article about it in the *Erie Ledger*. I suspect Evelyn knew someone at the home, and paid them handsomely to keep it quiet. She had her daughter admitted as Katrina Doe."

"Katz, people talk, especially in a small town. They gossip. Someone working at the home would have spilled the beans. But, if Evelyn paid off the person in charge, then they could have kept it secret."

"After the fire, which claimed the life of seven teenaged girls, it looks like the media would have had a field day with it, yet I only found one short article. The fire chief said the fire was accidental, end of story."

"Who knows," Jake said. "Maybe in the 1960s, the county government was corrupt. If the building wasn't kept up, all sorts of things could have caused the fire; faulty wiring is my number one guess."

"I'm surprised the other girls' parents didn't object."

"I'm thinking the other girls were from out-of-town, farmed here by parents who didn't give a damn, and then were forgotten."

"Jake, Stevie said his mother told him the babies were saved. But what happened to them?"

"Katz, I think the infants were adopted illegally, so there wouldn't be a record of it."

"How would Stevie's mother know this? The article in the newspaper said seven young women died, but didn't mention anything about their babies."

"Unfortunately, we can't ask her, because Stevie's mom passed away several years ago."

"Always a hurdle," she said, discouraged.

"If those adoptions were legal, the birth and adoption records are sealed."

"And the Home's copies of the adoption records — if there were any records — were destroyed in the fire."

Jake shook his head. "Katz, I don't mean to burst your bubble, but maybe this is the grave of another Katrina."

"But Jake, don't you find it odd that my missing shoes were on top of Katrina's grave?"

"Spooky, I agree, but . . . "

"I just wish I could find a picture of Katrina."

Jake rubbed his chin. "Umm, photo. I've got an idea. Let's drop Scout off at the Foursquare, and go have a look at the library."

"Why? The *Erie Ledger* is online."

"I know, but we're not looking at newspaper articles. We're looking for Erie school yearbooks, instead. Katz, you can at least find out if the ghost you've been seeing is *really* Katrina Clay. Her picture would be in the 1964 or 1965 yearbook."

"Brilliant!"

Scout nudged her head under Katherine's chin.

Katherine hugged her. "You knew all along, didn't you?" she asked the cat.

Scout crossed her eyes, and gave a deranged look.

"So that's my plan," Jake said.

"If I have it my way, all seven girls will be moved to the Ethel cemetery."

"That sounds like a difficult undertaking."

"No, you didn't just use that word."

"Oh, sorry. It won't be easy. I'm sure there will be lots of red tape, and legal hurdles to jump."

"That's why I have an attorney," Katherine smiled.

"What about this wreck of a building?"

"Demolish it! Bulldoze it! This land isn't that far from the Erie town limits. We could make it into a memorial park."

"That's not a bad idea. I think it will be easier for Erie to remember this place for the right reasons — what happened to these girls — if the building is torn down, and a memorial park is built. But, Katz, this will be expensive."

"It shouldn't cost too much," Katherine said, covering her mouth to conceal a laugh.

Jake winked, "Yeah, if you're a millionaire." He extracted his cell phone and clicked a picture of the grave marker. "Let's head on out, Sweet Pea. I'll carry Scout."

Katherine handed the Siamese to him. "Do you think Katrina's spirit will move on, once we bury her with her real name?"

"Let's make sure it's really Katrina Clay, first, okay?"

"Ma-waugh," Scout agreed.

Chapter Twenty-seven

Later that evening, a fast-moving thunderstorm swept through Erie, leaving behind fallen limbs and other kinds of storm debris. Jake and Cokey were at the pink mansion, framing out the new maintenance room in the basement.

Katherine nervously waited at the front door of the Foursquare for Colleen, who was fifteen minutes late. A second storm was pushing through with loud thunder and lightning. Then, the heavy rain began. Colleen parked in front of the Foursquare, opened her umbrella, and ran to the house. Katherine opened the door.

"Colleen, hurry up and come in. I was worried about you driving in this."

"Oh, I didn't drive from the city. I've been with Daryl."

"Did you two make up?" Katherine asked nosily.

Colleen didn't answer, but shifted the topic. "This rain just won't let up."

"It's better than snow," Katherine volunteered. "Where's your equipment?"

"I only brought the K2 meter and the flashlight this time. No need for the other stuff."

"Here, come to the kitchen. I've got something to show you."

"Where are the cats?" Colleen asked, looking around.

"Scout and Abra are prowling around, but I locked the others in a room upstairs. The kittens are back from their surgeries, and aren't supposed to be running around, but try to explain that to two hyperactive Siamese," Katherine chuckled.

"Katz, why don't Jake and you move into the bungalow while the mansion is being worked on? Mum and Jacky are back in Manhattan. Daryl and I can help you move your stuff."

"We don't have that much to move, but thanks for offering," Katherine said, then asked again. "That's the second time you've mentioned Daryl. Did you or didn't you get back together?"

"Yes, Katz, we did. Daryl said he was going to be more sensitive to my needs, instead of becoming Mr. Hyde when I disagree about something."

"Are you referring to what you told me happened at the armory?"

"I'm probably being a selfish brat, but I'd much rather have my boyfriend ask me instead of order me to do something."

"Yes, I agree. Colleen, I'm not taking sides here, but Daryl was probably trying to hide the fact that he was freaked out that his cousin Jake, and maybe even me, were at the mansion during the explosion."

"Speaking of Jake, where is he?"

"He's next door helping Cokey. As soon as they get the basement framing done, they can start hanging sheetrock."

"Jake has time for that with his teaching schedule?"

"No, I meant to say, Cokey and Margie have a drywall crew that will come in and finish."

"Okay, I get it now. You want to keep a close eye on the progress being made at the mansion."

"Something like that. Plus, to make sure Cokey doesn't leave anymore flammable rags around."

"Exactly, and also, that no one smokes in your house!" Colleen caught herself. "I'm sorry. That sounded really bad considering the fact my brother caused the fire."

"That's water under the bridge. For your brother's sake, I'm glad the fire chief ruled the explosion accidental. Jacky and I talked about what happened. I told him I would forgive him, if he'd seek help for his drinking problem."

"I pray he follows through. When did you talk to him?"

"Mum brought him by before they drove to the airport in Indy."

Colleen stopped, and put a finger to her lips. "Shhh, Katz, did you hear that?" She gazed up the stairs.

"Mao," Dewey cried. "Yowl," Iris answered, behind the closed door of the upstairs front bedroom.

"That's the cats. Jake and I made a cat room upstairs."

"Where, pray tell?" Colleen asked. "I hope it's not in the haunted rocking chair room."

"We haven't had a paranormal experience since Jake and I found Katrina's grave."

"Seriously?"

Katherine nodded.

The two walked to the kitchen, which was beautifully appointed with appliances, but lacked a dining table. Margie's and Cokey's folding card table with metal chairs were in the corner.

"Have a seat," Katherine said. "Want something to drink?"

Colleen sat down, and set her large bag on the oak floor. "No, I'm good."

Katherine slid a yearbook in front of Colleen. "Remember when I texted that Jake and I were heading to the library to look at Erie school yearbooks?"

"Yeah, is this one of them?"

"The library didn't have the year we wanted, but Jake's great-uncle, at the courthouse, loaned us his copy."

Katherine opened the yearbook to the page marked with a yellow post-it note.

Colleen moved closer to look. "Class of 1964," she read out loud. "Which one is it?"

Katherine pointed to the middle photo.

"Ah, she was so pretty."

"Meet our ghost — Katrina Evelyn Clay," Katherine announced solemnly.

"Spirit," Colleen corrected. "So, Katz, there isn't a reason for us to communicate with Katrina. She's passed over, and — "

"Is at peace now," Katherine finished.

"Do you think we'll ever find out why she warned you?"

"I don't think we'll ever know, but I thank Katrina for saving my life. She beckoned me to go into the carriage house, so I wouldn't be in the explosion."

Colleen agreed. "It makes good sense to me. Have you decided on a name for the memorial park?"

"Katrina's Park. I want it to be a happy place for children," Katherine said, breaking into a wide smile.

Scout and Abra slinked into the room, and assumed their stalking positions. They lowered their heads and crept slowly, their stomachs almost touching the floor. Abra's tail twitched furiously, while Scout's thumped back-and-forth, in an agitated fashion.

Scout clucked. "At-at-at-at."

"Girls, what is it?" Katherine whispered, slightly alarmed, thinking the spirit was back.

Colleen swiftly reached into her bag and extracted her K2 meter.

The Siamese continued stalking an unseen force, slowly and steadily, until Scout pounced on the object at hand — a small gray mouse. The mouse thwarted the great Siamese huntress by running underneath the refrigerator.

Colleen screamed, while Katherine jumped up on her chair. "A mouse!"

Abra glanced at Katherine, and licked her lips in tasty anticipation while Scout crossed her eyes dreamily.

Katherine got down from her chair, and caught each cat around the middle. "Oh, no, you don't. I'm taking you two upstairs."

Scout squawked, and Abra shrieked a loud "Raw" in protest.

Colleen leaped out of her chair, and said, "You're not leaving me alone in here with a mouse!"

The Siamese struggled to be put down. "Stop it! You're not catching that poor creature on my watch."

Colleen said, "You really want to stay here now?"

"Not thinkin' so," Katherine answered. "As soon as I put the cats in their room, I'm calling Jake. We're officially moving to the bungalow — tonight!"

"Na-waugh," Scout disagreed, and lightly bit Katherine on the chin. "Naw," Abra added.

The End

Dear Reader . . .

I love it when my readers write to me. If you'd like to email me about what you'd like to see in the next book, or just talk about your favorite scenes and characters, email me at: karenannegolden@gmail.com

Thank you so much for reading my book. I hope you enjoyed reading it as much as I did writing it. If you liked "*The Cats that Stalked a Ghost*," I would be so thankful if you'd help others enjoy this book, too, by recommending it to your friends, family, and book clubs, and/or by writing a positive review on Amazon and/or Goodreads.

I love to post pictures of my cats on my Facebook pages, and would enjoy learning about your pets, as well.

Follow me @
https://www.facebook.com/karenannegolden

Website: http://www.karenannegolden.webs.com

Amazon author page: http://tinyurl.com/mkmpg4d

Thanks again!

Karen

Acknowledgements

Thanks to my husband, Jeff, who is always the very first one to read my book.

Special thanks to Vicki Braun, my editor, who is a lot of fun to work with. Vicki also edited the first five books of *The Cats That . . .* Cozy Mystery series.

Also, thanks to Ramona Lockwood, my book cover designer.

Thank you to my beta readers: Linda Golden, Ramona Kekstadt, and Melissa McGee.

Thanks to my cats that keep me on my toes, and offer so much material for me to write about. Redmond, a ginger rescue, can open many locks. He throws books off my bookcase when he wants to chill out from the world. And, Rusty, a flame-point rescue, graces my Facebook pages with his funny antics.

At the Rainbow Bridge, special hugs to my Siamese cat, Princess Pee Wee, who inspired me to write the character of Scout. Also, Iris, who was a Siamese thief, and Lilac who really did cry "Me-yowl."

The Cats that Surfed the Web

Book One in *The Cats that* . . . Cozy Mystery series

If you haven't read the first book, *The Cats that Surfed the Web*, you can download the Kindle version on Amazon: http://amzn.com/B00H2862YG Paperback is also available.

With over 272 Amazon five-star reviews, "The Cats that Surfed the Web," is an action-packed, exhilarating read. When Katherine "Katz" Kendall, a career woman with cats, discovers she's the sole heir of a huge inheritance, she can't believe her good luck. She's okay with the conditions in the will: Move from New York City to the small town of Erie, Indiana, live in her great aunt's pink Victorian mansion, and take care of an Abyssinian cat. With her three Siamese cats and best friend Colleen riding shotgun, Katz leaves Manhattan to find a former housekeeper dead in the basement. There are people in the town who are furious that they didn't get the money. But who would be greedy enough to get rid of the rightful heir to take the money and run?

Four adventurous felines help Katz solve the crimes by mysteriously "searching" the Internet for clues. If you love cats, especially cozy cat mysteries, you'll enjoy this series.

The Cats that Chased the Storm

Book Two in *The Cats that . . .* Cozy Mystery series

The second book, *The Cats that Chased the Storm*, is also available on Kindle and in paperback. Amazon: http://amzn.com/B00IPOPJOU

It's early May in Erie, Indiana, and the weather has turned most foul. We find Katherine "Katz" Kendall, heiress to the Colfax fortune, living in a pink mansion, caring for her three Siamese and Abby the Abyssinian. Severe thunderstorms frighten the cats, but Scout is better than any weather app. A different storm is brewing, however, with a discovery that connects great-uncle William Colfax to the notorious gangster John Dillinger. Why is the Erie Historical Society so eager to get William's personal papers? Is the new man in Katherine's life a fortune hunter? Will Abra mysteriously reappear, and is Abby a magnet for danger?

A fast-paced whodunit, the second book in "The Cats that" series involves four extraordinary felines that help Katz unravel the mysteries in her life.

The Cats that Told a Fortune

Book Three in *The Cats that . . .* Cozy Mystery series

The third book, *The Cats that Told a Fortune*, is available on Kindle and in paperback. Amazon: http://amzn.com/B00MAAZ3ZU

With over 150 Amazon five-star reviews, "The Cats that Told a Fortune" is an action-packed, exhilarating read. In the land of corn mazes and covered bridge festivals, a serial killer is on the loose. Autumn in Erie, Indiana means cool days of intrigue and subterfuge. Katherine "Katz" Kendall settles into her late great aunt's Victorian mansion with her five cats. A Halloween party at the mansion turns out to be more than Katz planned for. Meanwhile, she's teaching her first computer training class, and a serial killer is murdering young women. Along the way, Katz and her cats uncover important clues to the identity of the killer, and find out about Erie's local crime family . . . the hard way.

The Cats that Played the Market

Book Four in *The Cats that* . . . Cozy Mystery series

If you haven't read the fourth book, *The Cats that Played the Market*, you can download the Kindle version or purchase the paperback on Amazon at: http://amzn.com/B00Q71LBYA

If you love mysteries with cats, don't miss this action-packed page turner. A blizzard blows into Indiana, bringing gifts, gala events, and a ghastly murder to heiress Katherine "Katz" Kendall. It's Katherine's birthday, and she gets more than she bargains for when someone evil from her past comes back to haunt her. After all hell breaks loose at the Erie Museum's opening, Katherine and her five cats unwittingly stumble upon clues that help solve a mystery. But has Scout lost her special abilities? Or will Katz find that another one of her amazing felines is a super-sleuth?

With the cats providing clues, it's up to Katherine and her friends to piece together the murderous puzzle . . . before the town goes bust! With over 123 five-star Amazon reviews, this thrilling, suspenseful read will keep you guessing until the last page.

The Cats that Watched the Woods

Book Five in *The Cats that . . .* Cozy Mystery series

If you haven't read the fifth book, *The Cats that Watched the Woods*, you can download the Kindle version or purchase the paperback on Amazon at:
http://amzn.com/B00VKF9Q2M

What have the extraordinary cats of millionaire Katherine "Katz" Kendall surfed up now? "Idyllic vacation cabin by a pond stocked with catfish." It's July in Erie, Indiana, and steamy weather fuels the tension between Katz and her fiancé, Jake. Katz rents the cabin for a private getaway, though Siamese cats, Scout and Abra, demand to go along. How does a peaceful, serene setting go south in such a hurry? Is the terrifying man in the woods real, or is he the legendary ghost of Peace Lake? It's up to Katz and her cats to piece together the mysterious puzzle. The fifth book in the popular "The Cats that . . . Cozy Mystery" series is a suspenseful, thrilling ride that will keep you on the edge of your seat.

Made in the USA
Middletown, DE
18 September 2015